1-07 CB 88D

NORELIUS COMMUNITY LIBRARY

S0-BZV-889

712-263-9355

DATE DUE

MAY 1 7 200 MAR 2 2 2010		
JUN 1 4 2007 MANOV 0 9 2010		
JUL 0 2 2007 NOV 2 6 2013		
JUL 1 9 2007 JUL 3 1 2007		
SEP 0 4 2007 OCT 2 4 2007		
NOV 0 8 2007 NOV 1 7 2009		

MT DEMCO 128-5046

AH

NORELIUS COMMUNITY LIBRARY
1403 1st Avenue South
DENISON, IOWA 51442
712-263-9355

ATASCOCITA GOLD

Other westerns by Kent Conwell:

Junction Flats Drifter
Promise to a Dead Man
Bowie's Silver
Angelina Showdown
Gunfight at Frio Canyon
An Eye for an Eye
A Hanging in Hidetown
The Gambling Man
Red River Crossing
A Wagon Train for Brides
Friday's Station
Sidetrip to Sand Springs
The Alamo Trail
Blood Brothers
The Gold of Black Mountain
Glitter of Gold
The Ghost of Blue Bone Mesa
Texas Orphan Train
Painted Comanche Tree
Valley of Gold
Bumpo, Bill, and the Girls
Wild Rose Pass
Cattle Drive to Dodge

The *Tony Boudreaux Mystery* Series:

Extracurricular Murder
The Ying on Triad
Skeletons of the Atchafalaya
Death in the Distillery
Vicksburg
Galveston

Other Mysteries by Kent Conwell:

The Riddle of Mystery Inn

NORELIUS COMMUNITY LIBRARY
1403 1st Avenue South
DENISON, IOWA 51442
712-263-9355

ATASCOCITA GOLD

•

Kent Conwell

AVALON BOOKS
NEW YORK

© Copyright 2007 by Kent Conwell
All rights reserved.
All the characters in this book are fictitious,
and any resemblance to actual persons,
living or dead, is purely coincidental.

Published by Thomas Bouregy & Co., Inc.
160 Madison Avenue, New York, NY 10016

Library of Congress Cataloging-in-Publication Data

Conwell, Kent.
    Atascocita gold / Kent Conwell.
        p. cm.
    ISBN 978-0-8034-9840-2 (hardcover : acid-free paper)
    I. Title.

PS3553.OS47A83   2007
813'.54—dc22

2007003750

PRINTED IN THE UNITED STATES OF AMERICA
ON ACID-FREE PAPER
BY HADDON CRAFTSMEN, BLOOMSBURG, PENNSYLVANIA

To my grandson, Mikey, and to Susan and Mike, his
parents, whose lives will never be the same.
And to my wife, Gayle.

Chapter One

Waving an I.O.U., Mad Tom Gristy bared his rotted teeth, leaned across the poker table, and snarled. "Around here, cowboy, we don't tolerate jaspers what try to weasel out of their gambling debts."

"Yeah," growled his partner, Dave Rynning, a thin-lipped, cold-eyed killer dressed in black.

Cursing his gambling habit once again, Josh Carson smiled amiably, hiding his nervousness. "You misunderstood me, boys. When I said I didn't have the cash, I meant on me. Don't worry. My partner has the cash to cover that chit." He glanced around the saloon. A grin popped on his slender face. "There he is over there at the bar. He just walked in. The big jasper. Tiny Hamilton."

Mad Tom kept his eyes on the younger cowpoke

1

while he spoke to his partner. "He over there, Rynning?"

Rynning turned his cold eyes to the bar, spotting a large cowpoke with shoulders wide as a singletree. "There's a big *hombre* over there wearing a cowhide vest. Just bellied up to the bar."

Josh pushed back from the table, anxious to buy himself a little room to operate if necessary. "That's him, boys. I'll just amble over and get your money."

Rough hands on his shoulders shoved him down in his chair. Josh glanced up to see half a dozen hard-faced *hombres* glaring at him. "Just you stay put, cowboy," growled Mad Tom. He scratched at the week-old beard on his floppy jowls with blunt fingernails caked with dirt.

Josh tensed, but stayed put, calling himself every name he could think of for getting himself into another set-to over his weakness for poker.

"Rynning," growled Mad Tom. "Why don't you mosey over and accommodate that jasper at the bar." It was an order, not a request.

With cold eyes, Rynning eyed his partner. He arched an eyebrow. "You get him. I'll keep this one company."

Mad Tom jerked around, glaring at the gunfighter. Josh sensed the tension between the two.

Like two ornery bulls, the hardcases locked eyes, measuring each other. Electricity crackled through the smoky air in the saloon. Finally, Mad Tom grunted and pushed to his feet. A smug sneer played over Rynning's thin lips.

Mad Tom lumbered across the sawdust floor and reached up to tap Tiny Hamilton on the shoulder.

The big man turned slowly, an affable grin on his face. He had to lower his head as Mad Tom spoke and hooked his thumb over his shoulder. Tiny glanced across the room and frowned. A look of disgust twisted his square face. He shook his head and pushed Mad Tom aside as he strode purposefully across the sawdust floor to the poker table.

He jerked to a halt. His eyes narrowed. "Don't tell me you went and done it again."

Shifting in his chair uncomfortably, the slender cowpoke grinned boyishly at his scowling partner. "I'm sorry, Tiny, but I had three queens. It was a good hand. I just couldn't . . ." His words faded out. "Well, you know."

Tiny's eyes blazed fire. He glared at Josh for several seconds, then grabbed a mug of beer from the table and, despite the owner's protests, downed it in one gulp and slammed the empty mug on the table. "Blast it, Josh. When are you going to learn?"

"This is it, Tiny. Honest. I've learned my lesson."

He removed his battered gray Stetson and ran his fingers through close-cropped hair dark as oiled leather. "I'll never sit down at another poker table. You can believe me this time."

Dave Rynning frowned, then snorted. "Hold on there, cowboy. This ain't no family get-together. You owe me money. I want it. Nobody runs out on a poker debt here in Atascocita. It ain't healthy." He cut his beady snake eyes from Josh to Tiny.

Shrugging his massive shoulders, Tiny shook his head and jammed a ham-sized hand in his pocket. "All right. How much?"

Mad Tom spoke up. "Seventy-eight dollars."

Tiny Hamilton froze, his hand halfway out of his pocket. He gaped at Mad Tom. "How much did you say, friend?"

The pot-bellied cowpoke sneered. "What's the matter, big man? You hard of hearing? I said seventy-eight dollars."

Tiny's massive body stiffened momentarily, then he relaxed. "Don't reckon I am, Mister, but I am some shy of seventy-eight dollars."

Several of the hardcases surrounding the table began to mutter. Dave Rynning waved for them to remain silent. His eyes narrowed. "Just how much shy?"

Pulling his hand from his pocket, Tiny plopped a handful of crumpled bills on the table with enough force to slosh some beer from the mugs. "About seventy dollars shy," he replied, staring hard at the gunfighter.

Rynning slowly rose to his feet, keeping his eyes on the cowpoke towering over him. He had never been intimidated by the size of an opponent. The matched Colts low on his hips always cut everyone down to size. He grinned crookedly at Tiny. "Well, then I suppose we'll just have to make up the difference some other way."

Behind him, a round of snickers rolled through the gathering of hardcases as they anticipated the fun.

"Yeah," one muttered.

"Let's go," mumbled another.

From where he was seated, Josh spoke up, a fist-sized knot of worry in the pit of his stomach. He had a sinking feeling things were about to go from bad to worse. "And how do you figure on making up the difference?"

His pallid face now a mask of pure innocence, Rynning turned to Josh. "Why, we're going to tar and feather you, then run your worthless carcasses out of town on a rail, that's how. Grab 'em, boys."

Before Josh or Tiny could move, a half-dozen waddies fell on them, pinning their arms behind their backs, but the hardcases had never confronted an *hombre* like Tiny Hamilton. With a mighty grunt, he swung both arms forward, jerking four surprised cowpokes off their feet and sending them sprawling onto the sawdust floor.

Taken aback momentarily, the two hardcases holding Josh loosened their grip, giving him the chance to yank free. He spun and slammed a knotted fist into Mad Tom's nose, smashing it all over his face. Suddenly, stars exploded in his head as the second cowpoke whopped him upside the temple.

Without warning, three gunshots cut through the riotous clamor of shouts and curses. "That's enough," a booming voice called out.

Josh shook his head to clear the cobwebs and realized he was still clutching Mad Tom's vest, ready to pop the bleeding jasper in the nose again. He released his grip and stepped back, trying to find the source of the gunshots.

Standing in front of the batwing doors, a medium-sized cowpoke wearing a black hat with a sombrero brim and a sugarloaf crown stood with a smoking six-shooter in his hand. His weathered face was grim, and his eyes cut into each of the offending cowboys like the knot on the tip of a braided rawhide bullwhip. On his chest glittered a star.

"You heard me, boys. And you know I don't say nothing twice." He eyed the suddenly silent mob of subdued cowpokes and then, revolver in hand, strode over to Dave Rynning. "What's going on here, Rynning? You know my law about fighting."

Rynning eyed the sheriff coldly. "It was them, Sheriff. The big one and that one over there by Mad Tom. They started it."

His jaw set, the sheriff surveyed the saloon. "Where's your other partner, Big Nose Crawford, and that fancy pearl handled six-gun he sports? He's usually right in the middle of your jamborees."

"He ain't here, Sheriff," Rynning replied. "Just me and Mad Tom." He jabbed a finger at Josh. "Now, what about them? They owe me."

Josh stepped forward. "That isn't the way it was, Sheriff. These old boys was all set to tar and feather my friend and me."

With a suspicious gleam in his eyes, the sheriff studied Josh. "You be a stranger in town, Mister. What's your name?"

"Josh Carson, Sheriff. This here big galoot is my partner, Tiny Hamilton, who is the great-grandson of Alexander Hamilton," he added, hoping the announcement would carry some weight with the sheriff. "We was just riding through this little town of yours when I thought—"

The sheriff cut him off sharply. "I didn't ask you that, cowboy. I asked your name. Now, if you and what's-his-name there want to stay on my good side, then you don't say nothing until I ask, and then you tell me only what I want to know, you hear?"

Josh glanced at Tiny, who nodded imperceptibly. "I understand, Sheriff," Josh replied.

Taking a deep breath, the sheriff holstered his six-gun and turned to Dave Rynning. "What do you have to say about that, Rynning?"

Eyes narrowing, Rynning shrugged. "That no-account was trying to beat us out of a poker bet, Sheriff. We just figured on having some fun with them two. That's all."

The sheriff grunted. He knew Rynning, and he knew the killer was lying. He looked up at Tiny Hamilton. "Is what he says right, cowboy?"

Tiny nodded. "Yes, sir. Josh there lost seventy-seven dollars and—"

"Seventy-eight," Mad Tom sputtered, still holding his nose with blood running through his fingers and dripping from his grizzled chin onto his dirt-stained shirt.

"Seventy-eight," Tiny said, correcting himself. "I only had eight dollars, so this one . . ." he explained, nodding to Rynning, "this one said they would make up the difference by tar and feathering us. And that's when the trouble started, Sheriff."

"Why was you paying your friend's gambling debts?" the sheriff asked. Before Tiny could answer, the sheriff frowned at Josh. "And what the blazes was you doing playing poker if you don't have no money?"

"Well, I—I thought I had it won, Sheriff, so I took a chance." Josh grimaced at his puny explanation.

"Josh knows better than to play poker, Sheriff," Tiny put in. "Once he gets started, he can't stop. It's a bad habit."

The sheriff arched an eyebrow. "Well, I reckon that's one habit I can stop." He hooked a thumb toward the batwing doors. "Let's go, you two. The hoosegow."

Dave Rynning spoke up. "What about my money, Sheriff? That jasper owes it. It ain't right letting him get away with that."

Sheriff Ellis snorted, "He ain't getting away with nothing, Rynning, just like you ain't fooling nobody about just funning around with these two. Atascocita needs sprucing up. I figure it'll cost about seventy dollars to clean things up around here."

Josh glanced up at Tiny, who wore a puzzled frown. "Sheriff, you mean, me and Tiny here is going—"

"I mean, you and Tiny here is going to jail. Daytime, you'll clean up the town. Nights, you'll enjoy the warm hospitality of the Atascocita hoosegow. Once you've paid your debt, I don't want to never see either of you two around here again. Now git."

"But, Sheriff," Josh sputtered. "What—"

Sheriff Ellis stepped up to Josh and jabbed the cowpoke in the chest with his forefinger. "Look, cowboy, I just stopped you and your big friend here from a ride on a hitching rail. You want that, or you want it my way?"

Tiny slammed the heel of his hand into Josh's shoulder, sending the smaller cowpoke stumbling. "Shut up, Josh. The sheriff here's right. Let's do what we got to do and leave this place behind."

Sheriff Ellis grinned up at Tiny. "Glad one of you old boys got some sense." He nodded to the door. "Let's go."

Aggravated, Josh shoved the batwing doors open, and promptly ran into Frenchy Buckalew, sending both of them tumbling from the boardwalk and sprawling in a tangle of arms and legs on the dusty streets of Atascocita.

Chapter Two

Frenchy Buckalew was of an age she refused to admit, but as the owner of the Buckalew Freight Line with her husband, George, she was a no-nonsense woman with a will of iron and a heart of gold.

But that didn't stop her from exploding into a string of profanity that would have made any bullwhacker blush. She came out of the tangle of arms and legs kicking and swearing. Pushing herself to her feet, she glared down at Josh Carson, her hat askew, her graying hair tangled, and her eyes spitting fire. She popped the quirt looped around her wrist against her heavy denim skirt. "What the Sam Hill is going on here?" She glanced up on the boardwalk at Tiny and the sheriff. "Dan Ellis, what do you think you're doing?"

11

The sheriff laughed and clambered down the steps. "Now, now, Frenchy. It was just an accident. I was taking these two over to the jail."

By now, Josh had jumped to his feet and removed his Stetson. He stammered, "Sorry, ma'am. I wasn't paying attention. I didn't mean to cause you no trouble. Are you hurt?"

She glared at him, but the motherly instinct took over when she saw just how contrite the young cowpoke was. She cackled and brushed the dust from her split skirt with the quirt. "Heavens, no, boy. I ain't hurt none. Takes more than a little tumble to bother me." She hesitated, then looked around at the sheriff. "You say you're taking these two to the hoosegow, Dan. Why, they don't look like no desperate criminals to me."

Sheriff Ellis chuckled. "They ain't, Frenchy. That one, the one you tangled up with, tried to welsh on a poker bet. Rynning and that bunch was figuring on giving them a new set of tar and feather duds, then helping them out of Atascocita on a hitching rail." He paused and drew a deep breath. Letting it out, he added. "Knowing Rynning and that bunch, it wouldn't have ended there, and then that would probably have caused a heap of trouble for me, so I figured on putting the two to work to pay off what they owe."

A thoughtful look came over her face. She touched the tip of the quirt to Josh's chest. "How much do you owe, boy?"

"Seventy dollars, ma'am."

She pointed the quirt at Tiny. "What about you?"

He grinned amiably. "I'm with him, ma'am. Good times and bad. Reckon this is one of the bad," he added sheepishly.

She laughed. "You boys know anything about oxen?"

Josh and Tiny exchanged puzzled looks. Josh nodded. "Yes, ma'am. Oxen, mules. Back home, we worked them in the fields."

"Good," she exclaimed. "Tell you what, Sheriff. I like these boys. George and me just lost a couple bullwhackers. I'll pay what these jaspers owe, and they can work it off for me. Save you the trouble of keeping them busy." Pursing her lips, she arched an eyebrow. "That is if you boys got no problems with that."

Tiny blurted out. "No, ma'am, we don't. Neither one of us."

She cut her eyes to Josh.

He grinned. "I'm with him, ma'am. Like he said, good times and bad."

"Well, Sheriff?" She faced him, her fists jammed into her ample hips.

Sheriff Dan Ellis shrugged. "Fine with me."

"Good. I'll be over in a few minutes with the cash." She spun on her heel. "Grab your ponies, boys, and follow me."

Leading his dun across the dusty street, Josh spoke up. "We sure are much obliged to you for bailing us out, ma'am. You sure won't regret it."

She called back over her shoulder. "I don't plan on regretting nothing, young fella. You'll work it off."

Tiny grinned down at Josh, but the tone in her voice gave the smaller cowpoke the feeling that they just might avoid a heap of trouble if they opted on jail instead.

She led them into a livery with the sign over the door that read *Buckalew's Livery and Freight.* "Over there's the office. Out back is the barn where we keep the oxen." She nodded to half a dozen or so stabled horses and pointed to some empty stalls. "You can put your ponies over there next to that gray mare, then come on to the office. I'll tell George you're coming. He's my husband. While you're taking care of that, I'll pay off your debt."

Minutes later, Josh and Tiny stood in front of a battered desk from behind which a bald-headed old man wrinkled like a fresh-plowed field looked up at them. "So," he said in a cackle. "I hear the old lady has talked you boys into working for us, huh?"

NORELIUS COMMUNITY LIBRARY
1403 1st Avenue South
DENISON, IOWA 51442

Josh started to set him straight, but Tiny replied first. "Yes, sir. And we appreciate the jobs. You won't be sorry."

The old man extended a crumpled hand severely knotted by arthritis. "I'm George, Frenchy's husband."

Shaking his hand gingerly, Josh and Tiny introduced themselves.

The back door of the office opened. Beyond, Josh saw a small kitchen. Their living quarters, Josh figured.

Frenchy strode in. "I see everyone knows everyone, so let's get down to business. First, you boys owe me seventy dollars. I figure a good bullwhacker is worth twenty a month, so in three months, you boys should have me paid off."

"Three months?" Josh frowned. But that's a hundred and twenty. We could pay you off what we owe in two months."

A knowing smile curled one side of her lips. "Ain't you boys figuring on eating? I hope you don't reckon I'm going to feed two growed men. Now, me and George don't mind if you throw your bedrolls up in the livery loft, but I figure it'll take you at least three months to settle up. What do you think?"

Josh studied her a moment, seeing something in her smiling eyes that dared him to argue with her. He chuckled.

"What's so funny," she demanded.

He shook his head. "Nothing, ma'am. I figure you got yourself two hard-working jaspers for the next three months. Right, Tiny?"

Tiny smiled amiably. "Yes, ma'am."

"One other thing." She fixed them with a challenging look. "There's another freight line in town run by a jasper called Cullen Leach. Them boys you had trouble with over in the saloon work for him. Leach wants to run me and George out of business."

"Ain't likely," George said, his thin voice trembling in anger.

Frenchy leaned over and laid a weathered hand covered with age spots on his twisted knuckles. "Take it easy, George. We're going to make it just fine. Ain't you always said that?" She looked back at Josh and Tiny. "All I'm saying is that there might be some trouble. You boys game?"

Josh studied a moment. He'd only known her a few minutes, but he felt drawn to her grit and resolve. "Yes, ma'am. I reckon we are."

"How about you, Tiny?" She had to look almost straight up to meet his eyes.

A crooked grin played over his lips. "Like I said before, ma'am. Josh and me are together through good and bad."

She smiled. "All right. Follow me. Like I said, the

oxen are out back in their barn. And," she added as she opened the door to the livery, "no smoking up in the loft."

That night in the loft, they rolled out their soogans on either side of a wooden keg turned upside down on which sat a barn lantern for light. Tiny stretched out on his blankets and groaned. "Feels mighty good to lie down."

"Yep," Josh muttered, rummaging through his saddlebags. "Going to be a hot night."

Tiny looked at the gaps in the board and batten walls of the livery and chuckled. "Well, at least we can count on a breeze to cool us some." He rolled over on his side. "Turn out the lantern when you're ready."

"I'm going to read awhile," Josh replied, pulling a book from his gear and lying back on his bedroll.

With a groan of resignation, Tiny grunted. "I figured so. Which one tonight?"

"Twenty Thousand Leagues Under the Sea."

His eyes closed, Tiny mumbled, "You know, you're going to wear them pages out, you read them so much. How many times you read that one?"

Josh glanced at his partner. His thoughts drifted back through the years. He and Tiny had grown up together in East Texas when Tiny had come to live

with Josh and his Pa at Injun Bayou after Tiny's Pa
had gone off to war. Josh's Pa soon followed, and
from then on, it was just the two boys keeping up the
home place. During all that time, Josh read books,
any books he could get his hands on. "I don't remember." He laughed. "Lost count, I suppose."

His only reply was a soft fluttering of Tiny's lips
as he began snoring. Josh grinned. He'd never known
a soul who could fall asleep as fast as his partner. He
lay back, ready to enjoy the adventures of Captain
Nemo and Ned Land once again. But Tiny was right.
The pages were worn just about as thin as Bull
Durham paper. Maybe next time he had a few pennies in his pocket, he would try to find one of those
new books by the writer jasper named Mark Twain.
From what he had heard, *The Adventures of Tom
Sawyer* was a real sidesplitter.

After an hour, Josh rubbed his knotted fists into
his eyes and slipped the book back in his saddlebags.
Wary of fire, he rose and hung the barn lantern on a
nearby support post before turning it out and feeling
his way back to his soogan.

Stretching out on his blankets, Josh laced his fingers together behind his head and stared into the darkness above. "No more, Lord," he whispered. "That's
the last poker game I'll sit in. That's a promise."

He rolled over on his side and, his conscience clear, promptly fell asleep.

It seemed like only seconds later when hands shook his roughly and a frantic voice cut into his sleep. "Josh. Get the blazes up. Fire! The barn's on fire!"

Instantly awake, Josh jerked erect, his first thought that the barn lantern he had hung on the post had fallen, but through the open door in the livery, he spotted flames from the ox barn leaping high into the dark sky. Above the roar of the fire came the frightened bellows of the trapped oxen.

He yanked on his boots and grabbed his gunbelt and hat. He felt the heat against his face.

"Get our horses out of the livery in case it goes up," he shouted, scooping up his soogan and tossing it to the ground below. He clambered down the ladder. "I'll get the oxen."

Josh raced across the corral and threw open the side door of the barn. Smoke poured out, and the heat slammed him in the face.

At that moment, Frenchy Buckalew stumbled from the office, a threadbare chenille house robe gathered about her thick waist. Josh waved her back, ducking his head against the heat. "We'll get the animals. Stay back," he instructed her.

By now flames were eating through the roof of the barn.

She shouted above the roar of the fire. "Go around to the back. Open the back door of the barn. You can get them out that way."

His lungs burning from the thick smoke, Josh raced to the rear of the barn and tried to throw open the double doors, but flames licking through the cracks drove him back. Inside, the oxen bellowed frantically.

To his horror, Josh saw that by now, the entire barn was almost engulfed in flames. He ran back into the livery, grabbed his blanket, immersed it in the water trough and, slinging it over his head, sprinted to the rear doors. Using the wet blanket as a shield, he managed to throw open the swinging doors.

Seeing a means of escape from the raging inferno, the terrified oxen bolted through the door, knocking Josh aside and slamming him to the ground. When the lanky cowpoke hit the ground, he kept rolling, hoping to escape the sharp hooves of the frightened animals.

Suddenly, a powerful blow caught him in the back of the head, stunning him.

Inside the livery, Tiny freed the horses, driving them out, all except the gray mare who pawed at the air and squealed in terror, its eyes rolling in fear. After dodging her flailing hooves, he managed to un-snap her tie rope, and she bolted into the night.

Stunned, Josh struggled to sit up. Frenchy slipped her hands under his arms and half-dragged him away from the barn, which was now totally engulfed in flames.

Tiny rushed up. "The animals are all out." He knelt by Josh. "You all right, partner?"

Josh struggled to his feet, feeling himself gingerly. "I think so. Nothing seems busted."

"That was close." Tiny backed away from the searing flames. "This one's gone. Cross your fingers it don't set the livery on fire."

Frenchy set her jaw. "It won't if we wet it down."

By now, several townspeople had gathered and a bucket brigade was set up to soak the livery wall closest to the burning barn.

As quickly as the fire had ravaged the barn, it burned out, leaving only the charred remains in a heap of dancing sparks and slowly dying tongues of flames.

Eyes burning from the smoke, Josh stared at the smoking remains of the barn, for some reason feeling a strange sense of loss. "I'm sure sorry, ma'am," he said to Frenchy, who was standing at his side. "If we'd seen it sooner, maybe we could have put it out."

Sheriff Ellis came to stand beside them. "What caused it, Frenchy? Someone leave a lantern burning?"

Josh saw the anger stiffen her jaw as she looked up at the sheriff. "I reckon someone did, Dan. And I reckon you know who that someone was."

Across the street, three men watched from a darkened window as the last of the charred ruins smoldered. Mad Tom grunted. "We done all right, huh, Mr. Leach?"

Cullen Leach hooked his thumbs in his vest. "Yep. Reckon you did." Now he figured it was time to put the second part of his plan into play. "Tom, you know Sosthenes Archiveque. I want you to find him for me. Tell him I've got a business offer."

Mad Tom frowned at his partner, Big Nose Crawford, curious as to why his boss wanted the murdering Comanchero, but smart enough not to ask. "Right away, Mr. Leach."

Chapter Three

The next morning, Josh and Tiny sat at a table in Rosie's Café with Frenchy, sipping coffee and staring out the window at the still smoldering ruins of the barn. In the corral surrounding the barn, several of the animals that had been saved milled about.

Tiny nodded to the gray mare. "Looks like that mare's calmed down. I ain't never seen one as spooked as she was last night. Why, I didn't know if I was going to get her out or not. She almost kicked me in the head two or three times."

Josh glanced at the deep-chested gray. From where he was sitting, the animal looked sound, though she still seemed spooked, shying at every puff of smoke that slipped up through the pile of smoking coals.

With a deep sigh, Frenchy leaned back in her chair and groaned. "Well, boys, it looks like the freight business is over with. Most of the oxen were burned so bad, the only Christian act was to put them out of their misery."

Rosie, a slight woman with her graying hair pulled back in a bun, refilled their coffee. "Want something to eat, Frenchy? I can whip up some hotcakes right fast."

Frenchy shook her head, her eyes filled with despair. "I ain't hungry, Rosie, but thanks anyway."

Rosie glanced at Josh and Tiny. They shook their heads. She smiled briefly. "Just let me know if you change your minds. You might think better on a full stomach."

After Rosie left, Frenchy shook her head, and tears glittered in her eyes. Speaking more to herself than Josh and Tiny, she muttered, "I don't know how he did it, but Cullen Leach is the one behind last night. I know it as sure as I know my name is Frenchy Buckalew." She stared unseeing at the smoldering pile of charred lumber that had been her barn.

An uncomfortable silence fell over the table. After a few minutes, Frenchy shook her head, jerking herself back to the present. She focused her eyes on Josh and Tiny. "Well, boys, I reckon you're out of job. No oxen, no freight line, and we had a big freight order from the Gaston Ranch to bring in from Dodge." She sighed heavily. "Well, reckon you might as well ride on out. I'll make it right with the sheriff."

Josh and Tiny exchanged puzzled looks. Josh cleared his throat. "There's bound to be something we can do to help, ma'am."

She chuckled ruefully. "What? Without the freight line, all the old man and me got left is the livery. And that sure won't support four of us. No, boys, were I you, I'd tie my soogans behind my saddle and light a shuck out of Atascocita."

An idea hit Josh. He cleared his throat. "I figure on talking to the sheriff, ma'am. Maybe he'll give you back your money if Tiny and me will clean up the town for him like he first said. It's only been one day."

Her eyes softened, but she snorted. "What's done is done. You boys ride out, you hear?"

Before Josh could protest, Tiny tapped him on the arm and nodded to the front door. "Out there," the big cowpoke whispered.

Josh followed Tiny out onto the boardwalk in front of the café. He frowned up at his partner. "What's on your mind that you couldn't say in there?"

Excited, Tiny blurted out his idea, the words tumbling over each other. "Look, I sure like that lady in there. She's done us both a big favor."

Josh frowned, trying to guess what Tiny had on his mind. "I like her too. So?"

"So, here's what we can do to help her out. Let's us ride over to Hidetown, get a couple odd jobs and pick up some cash. Now, I know that I gripe at you about your poker playing, but this is different. We pick up a few dollars over there, enough so you get in a poker game. Maybe you'll get lucky and win enough to come back over here and put Frenchy and George back in business. What do you think?"

Josh couldn't think. All he could do was gape up at his deranged partner. Finally, he found his voice. "What? Why, you don't have the brains of a grasshopper. Poker's what got us into this mess. Besides, I promised I wouldn't play no more poker."

Tiny shrugged his massive shoulders. "I won't hold you to it. Not this time."

Clearing his throat, Josh glanced around uncomfortably. In a whisper, he replied, "Well, I promised somebody else too."

"Huh?" Tiny frowned. "Who?" Then his face lit with exasperation. "Oh. You promised the Lord again, didn't you?"

Growing defensive, Josh shot back. "Yeah. So what?"

Shaking his head wearily, Tiny replied, "Look,

partner. You know I ain't bad-mouthing that, but be honest. You've done promised Him two hundred times you'd quit gambling, and you're still doing it." He blew out through his lips. "I just don't see what harm backsliding one more time would hurt. And if we could help Frenchy and George out, I don't reckon He would mind one bit."

Before Josh could reply, a dour-faced man with floppy jowls and wearing a business suit climbed the steps to the boardwalk and jostled Tiny aside as he entered the café.

Tiny's temper flared at the jasper's bad manners, but after a couple minutes, Josh calmed him. "We got enough problems without you breaking some ill-mannered *hombre* up."

Calming down, Tiny nodded. "I reckon you're right. Now, what about Hidetown? Unless you can figure out some other way to come up with cash for three or four spans of oxen."

Before Josh could respond, the café door jerked open, and the same bad-mannered jasper that had entered moments before emerged red-faced and sputtering.

"Wonder who that is," Tiny whispered, watching the angry man stride across the street, kicking up balloons of dust with each step.

"One way to find out. Let's go back inside. But whatever's going on, I'm not going to play another hand of poker, and that's final."

Tiny snorted and followed Josh inside.

"Cullen Leach," announced Frenchy. "He's the one trying to drive me out of business, and the one I figure was behind the fire last night."

"What did he want?"

She looked up at Josh and grinned wryly. "Why, to buy me out. What else?" She turned up her cup, but it was empty. She held it up, and Rosie hurried over. "Yep, he came in to tell me how sorry he was in one breath, and in the next, that he wanted to buy me out for pennies on the dollar, just like he's been doing other folks ever since he come in here three or four years back."

Glancing out the window at the livery, Tiny spotted the freight wagons in front of the livery. "Ain't there no way you can borrow the money for some oxen? Someone around here is bound to be willing give you a loan."

Frenchy and Rosie exchanged wry grins as the slight woman filled their cups. "Cullen has everything tied up, except me, and Rosie here."

Josh shook his head. "Shame."

Rosie hesitated in pouring. A tiny frown wrinkled

her forehead. "I just remembered something. Don't you still have them mules out at your pasture, Frenchy? You know, the ones you used before the oxen."

Sipping her coffee, Frenchy nodded. "Them worthless knotheads? What about them?"

An animated grin leaped to the slender woman's lips. "Use them instead of the oxen."

Excited, Josh spoke up. "You got mules?"

The older woman rolled her eyes. "If that's what you want to call them. Eighteen or twenty at last count. Some might have died, but what's there is running wild out at our pasture in Blue Buck Canyon. Used them before we got the oxen. None of them ain't seen a harness for the last four or five years. Can't even catch them no more."

Tiny slapped Josh on the shoulder. "You hear that?"

Frenchy frowned at them. "What the Sam Hill are you talking about?"

"Just this, Frenchy," said Josh. "Like we told you yesterday, me and Tiny here, we know mules. Oxen too. Cut our teeth on them growing up back in East Texas. We can bring them in. You got rigs for them?"

"Yes, ma'am," Tiny said. "Mules are just about as good as oxen pulling freight. Faster, and they can graze the grass along the way like them oxen do."

"What did you use on the mules, Missus Frenchy, reins or jerk-line?"

"Jerk-line." A frown deepened the wrinkles in her forehead. "But, you can't catch them ornery critters, and even if you did, it'll take a month to break them."

Josh chuckled and winked at Tiny. "Not if they've been broke before. You say you used them to haul freight before you got your oxen?"

For the first time that morning, a ray of hope filled Frenchy's eyes. She looked from one to the other. "You boys really believe you can do it? I mean, catch them mules and break them to harness. We only got three weeks to pick up the shipment at Dodge City or we lose the contract to Cullen Leach."

Tilting his battered Stetson to the back of his head, Josh drawled, "Just whereabouts is this Blue Buck Canyon, ma'am?"

A box canyon with a stone fence blocking the mouth, Blue Buck Canyon was an hour west of Atascocita near the caprock, a rugged wall rising over a hundred feet from the rolling sandhills of the Staked Plains.

Astride his dun at the gate, which was three rails of peeled cottonwood, Josh studied the canyon. It appeared about a mile wide and at least that deep. Lush blue grama grew belly-deep, dotted with patches of shinnery, stunted oak wrist thick and head high. Several giant cottonwoods grew in the middle of the canyon around a pond of clear artesian water.

Tiny whistled. "I hate to say this, old friend, but there ain't no way we're going to catch them mules, break them to harness, and be in Dodge City in three weeks. Why, best I recollect, it's over two hundred miles up there."

Josh removed his broad-brimmed hat and dragged the sleeve of his cotton shirt across his sweaty forehead. "Don't be too sure. You remember old man Tillotson back in Injun Bayou?"

Frowning momentarily, Tiny finally nodded. He shifted around in his saddle and pulled out a bag of Bull Durham and built a cigarette, then tossed Josh the bag. "What about him?"

Josh built his own cigarette and wearing a sneaky grin, continued, "Well, old Tillotson raised mules. He let them run wild through the woods, but he always brought in a heap of them every spring to sell."

Tiny touched a lucifer to his cigarette. "Yeah, now I remember. He always used a gray mule as a bell mule. What did he call it, Ulysses? After some jasper back in the old days across the oceans, he claimed."

The grin on Josh's face grew wider. "Ulysses? I'd forgotten that."

"I remember because I never could understand what he meant."

Josh snorted and teased his partner. "That's why you ought to read more, Tiny, so you won't be so ignorant. Ulysses was a Greek jasper that traveled all over the world and got himself out of all sorts of trouble. Anybody knows that."

"Well, I don't." A frown wrinkled the larger cowpoke's broad forehead. "Besides we ain't got a gray mule."

"No, we don't." Josh took a deep drag off his cigarette and let the smoke drift up into the clear sky. "But we got us a gray horse. Remember that mare that almost kicked you in the head last night?"

Tiny's eyes lit in understanding. "What are we waiting for?" he exclaimed, wheeling his blood bay pony about.

Chapter Four

While Tiny rummaged up a cowbell at Drayton's General Store, Josh threw a loop over the gray mare's head. The still frightened animal jerked against the taut rope several times before settling down and following without resistance. He rode up to Frenchy and George who were standing in the door to the livery, both their faces wreathed in puzzlement.

Josh grinned. "You find the harnesses?"

George pointed a trembling finger at a tangle of leather straps hanging on the back wall of the livery. "Twenty rigs. Need some repair. Ain't been used in five years or so."

Tiny rode up, the cowbell dangling from his saddle horn. "You ready?"

"Just you two hold on there," demanded Frenchy,

taking a few steps forward. "You boys ain't going nowhere until you tell us just what you got up your sleeve." Her eyes glittered with determination.

Josh chuckled. "Here's our plan, Missus Frenchy. No one knows why, but if there's a gray mule in a herd, all the others will follow it."

"He's right, ma'am," Tiny chimed in. "I've seen it."

She looked at them like they had lost their senses. "So what?"

"So, we're going to put a cowbell around this gray mare's neck and turn her into the canyon. In the next three or four days, those mules of yours will be following after her just like little puppy dogs."

George Buckalew cackled. "I been around horses and mules all my life, and I ain't never heard that."

Josh shrugged. "It'll work."

"What if it don't?" Frenchy said.

"Then we're no worse off than we are now."

She and George looked at each other, and the old man waved a knotted hand. "The boy's right, Frenchy. We won't be no worse off than we are now."

As Josh and Tiny neared Blue Buck Canyon, Tiny cleared his throat. "Getting the mules to tag after this mare ain't no problem, Josh. The problem is getting them all back to town. Wild mules ain't going to follow after no mare that's being led by a couple cow-pokes. Why, they'll scatter like quail soon as they leave the canyon."

"Not if they're running all out."

Tiny shifted around in his saddle and studied Josh. "What are you talking about?"

Josh pursed his lips. "I've been thinking."

"Uh-oh," Tiny grunted with a crooked grin. "That ain't good."

Ignoring his partner's jibe, the lanky cowpoke continued. "We'll find out if I'm right as soon as we turn her loose in the canyon."

Shrugging his wide shoulders, Tiny frowned. "Right about what?"

"Don't worry. You'll see."

Disgusted at his partner's reticence, Tiny blew out through his lips and reached in his vest pocket for his bag of Bull Durham.

Josh stopped him. "Not now. Wait until we get there."

Holding the bag of makings in his hand, Tiny glared at Josh. "Why not? What's it going to hurt?"

"We're almost there. Just wait. You'll see what I'm talking about."

Tiny arched an eyebrow. "Is this part of your plan?"

"More or less." Josh nodded. "More or less."

"It'd better be good," Tiny exclaimed, jamming the Bull Durham back in his vest.

Ten minutes later, they pulled up at the gate. Josh handed Tiny the lead rope. "Hold her while I put the bell on her."

Deftly, he made a couple loops about her neck with a stretch of rope and fastened the cowbell to it. "Now, open the gate."

With a skeptical look on his face, Tiny leaned down from his saddle and removed the top two rails.

His forefinger hooked around the bridle, Josh led the gray mare inside, closing the gate behind him. He halted and grinned up at Tiny. "Now, build your cigarette."

Thoroughly puzzled by his partner's request, he shook his head and quickly rolled a cigarette, then pulled out a lucifer.

Josh stopped him. "Ride up to the fence before you light it."

"Huh? What—"

"I want the mare to see the fire."

Still perplexed, Tiny did as Josh asked. He held the match next to the handle of his .44 caliber Remington. "All right. Can I light it now, Mr. Carson?"

"And don't cup the match in your hand. I want her to see the flame."

With a shrug, Tiny struck the match. It flared, and as he lifted it to his cigarette, the mare squealed and reared up, pawing frantically at the sky, jerking loose from Josh's grip on her bridle.

Josh dived over the gate. When he looked up the mare was racing through the lush grass, mane flying, her tail streaming out behind, and the cowbell clattering like a Philadelphia fire engine. He chuckled and looked up at Tiny.

Tiny shook his head. "What did that prove? She's scared of fire. Why wouldn't she be after last night?"

Climbing back in the saddle, Josh reined his dun around. "We'll give them three or four days to get used to the bell. I figure if we build a fire behind her, that'll drive her out of the canyon and the mules will follow."

Tiny raised a skeptical eyebrow.

Josh continued, "Once they leave the pasture, you and me have got to be right with them, you on one side and me on the other. She'll be scared and running hard. We got to keep pushing them. Once we tire out the mules, they won't think about scattering. They'll just follow the mare on in."

For several seconds, Tiny studied his partner. He drew a deep breath and shook his head. "Well, I'll swan, Josh. If that ain't sneaky, then I don't know what sneaky is."

* * *

The next morning Cullen Leach watched from the window of C. L. Freight as the two cowboys rode out of town. He spoke over his shoulder to Big Nose Crawford and Dave Rynning. "Follow those two. Find out what they're up to. This is the second day they've headed out west."

Crawford nodded, shucking his pearl-handled six-gun and checking the cylinder.

"And no shooting," Leach barked. "You hear me?"

Upon reaching the canyon, Josh and Tiny set about building four head-high piles of dried logs and branches mixed with tumbleweeds in the middle of the valley. From time to time as they dragged logs to the growing piles, they heard the ringing of the bell and spotted the mare. With a grin, Josh counted three mules trotting after her.

"Looks like it's working, huh?" Tiny muttered, dragging his sleeve across his sweaty forehead.

"Yep." Josh nodded. "Just like we figured."

Back in town, Cullen Leach looked up from his desk at C. L. Freight when Crawford and Rynning shoved open the door. "Well," Leach snarled, his fat fingers clutching an ink pen. He was still upset over Frenchy's turning down his offer to buy her out. "What did you find out? What are them two jaspers up to?"

Crawford shrugged. "Nothing that makes no sense, Mr. Leach."

Rynning shook his head. "It don't make no sense at all, Mr. Leach."

Leach felt his frustration growing, and his temper ready to explode. "Well, do I have to sit here all day, or are you going to tell me what's going on?"

Crawford's eyes glittered in anger momentarily, then softened in deference to his boss. "They're building piles of dry timber across the middle of the Blue Buck Canyon, like they was going to make some fires."

"That's right," Rynning said softly. "They're stacking wood for a fire."

"Huh?" Leach frowned, eyeing Crawford suspiciously. "They're doing what?"

Crawford glanced at Rynning for moral support, then replied, "He's right, Mr. Leach. Looks like they're going to build three or four fires in the middle of the canyon. That's what I meant when I say it didn't make no sense what they is up to."

Leach studied Crawford and Rynning several moments, wondering if they'd really followed the two jaspers out to Blue Buck Canyon or had spent the afternoon at the Atascocita Saloon. No, he told himself. Crawford was too dumb to not follow Leach's orders. His thick brain would never entertain the idea of any kind of deception. But Rynning . . . well, Rynning was a different cut of cloth. He was too quiet. A jasper never knew what was on the quiet man's mind.

"You want us to go back out and keep an eye out, Mr. Leach?" Crawford shuffled his feet nervously.

Leach shook his head and stared out the window at the passing wagons on the street. "Let's just wait and see what happens. You boys go on over to the saloon and wash the dust from your throats."

That night in the livery office, Josh explained the plan to Frenchy and George. "The mules are following the mare. Let's give them a couple more days. When we ride out, give us around three hours, and then start watching for us. We should have them tired out good and proper when we come in, but to be on the safe side, Missus Frenchy, when you see us coming, you might have to stand in the street to turn the mare into the corral. I figure she'll be worn to a nub just like the mules, but you can't tell."

Frenchy patted stray strands of gray hair back into place and rose and went into the kitchen, returning moments later with a pot of coffee, four mugs, and a half-full bottle of Old Orchard Whiskey. "Well, boys, I don't know if we should be celebrating or pitying each other. All I know is that if this wild scheme doesn't pan out, then Atascocita has seen the last of Buckalew Freight Lines."

Chapter Five

The next two days and nights, the four busied themselves repairing harnesses, splicing reins, traces, jerk-lines, rubbing grease and tallow into the collars to soften them, and inspecting chains and O-rings. When Josh was satisfied with the rigging for the animals, he and Tiny removed the wagon tongue with the neck yoke for oxen and replaced it with the chain to accommodate singletrees.

The next morning, Frenchy came into the livery carrying four jars of coal oil as Josh was saddling his dun. "Here's the coal oil for the fire."

Josh nodded. "Thanks," he replied, slipping the jars into his saddlebags and tying the flaps down.

"Everything's all set, huh?"

He snugged the cinch down tight on his center-fire rig and adjusted the stirrups. "Just about." He swung into the saddle, his right hand instinctively making sure the leather loop was securely around the hammer of his Colt .44. "Give us three hours or so. I don't know how we'll come in. I hope if we run them four or five miles, we'll wear them out so that they'll be too tired to do anything but follow the mare."

From outside, Tiny shouted, "Let's us go, Josh. The sun ain't getting any lower."

Frenchy took a step forward and laid a wrinkled hand on his knee. Her ever-present quirt dangled from her wrist. "You boys take care. This old freight line ain't worth nobody getting bad hurt."

A warm feeling swept over Josh. He grinned. "Don't worry, ma'am. We might not look it, but me and Tiny have been up and down the river a heap of times. We'll be just fine."

Cullen Leach watched from his window as the two cowpokes rode out of town. Big Nose Crawford stood at his shoulder. Leach pulled a cigar from his vest pocket. "Follow them. Keep an eye on what kind of tricks they're up to now."

Five minutes later, Big Nose Crawford, forking his

Spanish saddle astride a large sorrel, rode west out of town on the trail of Josh and Tiny.

From inside the livery, George called out. "Old lady. Come out here."

Frenchy stuck her head out the office door. "What do you want, old man?"

He waved a knotted hand down the street. "Big Nose Crawford just rode out of town in the same direction the boys went."

Her eyes narrowing, Frenchy came to stand at her husband's side, watching Crawford disappear around the adobe walls of the Atascocita Saloon.

George scratched his thinning hair. "What do you reckon he's up to?"

Frenchy shook her head. "Whatever it is, it's no good. You can bet on that."

Five minutes after the old couple returned to their office, Mad Tom Gristy tied up at the hitching rail in front of Leach's freight line.

Mad Tom lumbered into the office. "I found Archiveque, Mr. Leach. Where do you want to meet up with him? He's over to the Canadian River back east. He ain't none too anxious to show up in in Atascocita."

Nodding slowly, Leach replied, "That grove of cottonwoods where the river makes an oxbow back to the north. Have him there tonight around midnight."

"Yes, sir."

Leach sat staring at the door after his gunnie closed it behind him. First the Buckalew Freight Line and next the Gaston Ranch. It was the finest piece of property for fifty miles around, fit for a man of the stature of Cullen Leach, who one day would lord over a thousand sections of land, six hundred and forty thousand acres.

At Blue Buck Canyon Josh leaned from his saddle and dropped a couple rails from the gate so they could enter the canyon. Tiny replaced the rails behind them.

Josh glanced at Tiny and drew a deep breath. "How about it, partner? You ready to buck the tiger?"

Tiny tugged his John B down over his head and nodded. "Might as well."

"Here you go," the slender cowboy said, fishing two jars of coal oil from his saddlebags and handing them to Tiny.

With a wry grin, Tiny fit the jars in his saddlebags and glanced at the sun. "Looks like it's going to be hot enough to sunburn a horned toad today."

Josh chuckled. "It's going to get hotter." He nodded to the north wall of the canyon. "You head up that side. I'll take the other. Remember, we'll drive them toward the gate. Once they move far enough down the canyon, we'll fire the wood. The mare will run. With no way to get out, she'll run around the outside of the pasture looking for a way out. We'll let them circle the canyon a couple times before we throw down the gate. We'll be outside waiting for them."

Tiny shook his head and gave his partner a crooked grin. "This is a crazy idea, you know."

Josh lifted an eyebrow. "No crazier than you trying to talk me into a poker game."

For a brief moment, the two partners' eyes met. A slow smile played over their lips, and then they wheeled their ponies around.

"Let's get it done," shouted Tiny.

Josh crossed his fingers.

Josh held his dun in a walking two-step along the canyon wall. Halfway into the canyon, he heard the clanging of the cowbell as it moved toward the center of the canyon. And then he spotted the mare emerge from behind a patch of oak shinnery.

He suppressed a shout of glee and a grin leaped to his lips when he spotted over a dozen mules tagging after her.

"Now, go easy, Tiny," he muttered. "Get on behind them, then slow and careful like drive them toward the gate."

As the two cowpokes pushed the animals toward the gate, the mare stopped and looked back two or three times, curious as to who was behind her. Josh and Tiny made no sudden moves, just continued walking their ponies toward them.

Finally, the herd, which had picked up five or six more mules, passed the middle of the canyon.

Josh pulled up at the first pile of dried wood. A quarter of a mile across the canyon, Tiny waved at him. Josh waved back, pulled his Stetson down on his head snugly, and smashed the jar of coal oil on the logs. He struck a lucifer on the handle of his Colt and tossed it onto the wood. A tiny flame leaped up, and Josh dug his heels into the dun, racing toward the next stack of wood.

Two minutes later, four fires raged, leaping high into the clear sky.

As Josh cut his dun back toward the mules, he heard a loud squeal followed by the steady clanging of the cowbell.

At least the first part of his plan was working. The fires had frightened the mare, and she had bolted away from the inferno, directly for the closed gate.

Josh looked around at a loud hoorah and spotted Tiny standing in the stirrups of his galloping blood bay and waving his Stetson over his head.

The two pulled up at the gate as the mare led the mules around the perimeter of the box canyon, searching frantically for a means of escape from the fire.

Earlier, Big Nose Crawford had tied his sorrel in a clump of mesquite next to a large boulder a short piece from the gate and approached on foot. Wrinkling his nose at the acrid smell of wood smoke, he stood on tiptoe, but he couldn't see more than a couple hundred yards into the canyon because of the thick smoke drifting his way. He clambered up on the rock fence for a better view.

Suddenly, he heard the thundering of hooves. He peered into the smoke.

Without warning, the stampeding herd of mules burst from the smoke, heading directly for him. Behind them, he spotted two riders.

He lunged backward off the fence, slamming to the hard ground on his back. Stars exploded in his head. Groggily, he scrambled on his hands and knees back to the mesquite behind which he had tied his sorrel. He crouched and watched the animals sweep past the closed gate and disappear back into the smoke. The two cowpokes rode out of the pasture, replacing the rails behind them, then turned to peer into the smoke.

He frowned, trying to figure out just what those jaspers were up to. A couple minutes later, the animals thundered past the closed gate once again. After they passed, the big man leaned over from his saddle and easily yanked out the top two rails of the gate.

Big Nose's frown deepened as the two separated, one on either side of the open gate.

Minutes later, the ground vibrated once again with the pounding of hooves, and suddenly, through the thick curtain of acrid smoke, a gray mare followed by more than a dozen frightened mules burst through the open gate, thundering directly toward him.

Big Nose's eyes bugged open. In panic, the frightened hardcase threw himself behind the boulder, rolling up in a ball and covering his head.

The terrified animals rumbled past. As suddenly as they had appeared, the animals were gone, racing down the road toward Atascocita.

Big Nose's sorrel, frightened by the stampeding mules, tore loose and joined in the melee of animals racing down the road.

And right behind them came Josh and Tiny, slapping their Stetsons against their animals' flanks and shouting at the top of their lungs.

Standing high in his stirrups, Josh squinted into the smoke and dust-filled air, crossing his fingers that the mare would stay on the trail. He moved out to flank the stampeding herd just in case the mare did try to bolt.

After twenty minutes of breakneck galloping, the mare began to slow. Josh clenched his teeth, hoping the mules would do likewise.

Finally, a mile west of Atascocita, the mare slowed to a walk, the cowbell still clanging, and to Josh's relief, the mules fell in behind her, too tired to do anything but plod along after the bell mare.

Gesturing to the sorrel carrying an empty, but fancy silver inlaid saddle, Tiny called across the file of plodding animals. "Where'd that horse come from?"

Josh shook his head. "It joined up back at the canyon."

Fifteen minutes later, Frenchy closed the corral gate behind the mules while George stood in the livery door shaking his head. "I never would have believed it," he muttered, eyeing the gray mare. "I don't reckon a jasper's never too old to learn something."

Across the street inside C. L. Freight, Dave Rynning pointed to the corral. "Best take a look at this, Mr. Leach. Them jaspers done brought in a herd of mules."

"They what?" Leach pushed to his feet and lumbered to the window. He studied the milling animals and scratched his head. "You don't suppose—"

While he was puzzling at what was going on, the corral gate opened and Josh led a saddled pony out. For a few moments, Frenchy and Josh were engaged in a conversation. Her husband hobbled up, and the two of them studied the horse. Frenchy then pointed across the street in the direction of C. L. Freight.

Rynning exclaimed. "Hey, ain't that Big Nose's sorrel that come in with them mules?"

Leach peered through the window. "How in the blazes did it get in there? And where is Crawford?"

"That jasper who tried to welsh on his bet is bringing the sorrel over here," Rynning muttered.

Gesturing to the door, Leach barked, "Go out there and meet him. Find out what happened."

Rynning spoke up. "You don't reckon they bushwhacked him?"

Jowls flopping, Leach shook his head. "Don't be an idiot. Of course not."

Rynning's eyes blazed momentarily, then the fire died out and he went outside to meet Josh.

Leach looked on as the slender cowboy spoke with Rynning and pointed west. Rynning turned to come back inside.

* * *

"All that jasper knows, Mr. Leach, is that Big Nose's sorrel just joined in with the herd on the way to town from Blue Buck Canyon. Frenchy told him to bring it over."

Leach frowned. "He didn't see Crawford?"

Rynning grunted. "Says he didn't."

After another few moments pondering the enigma of the missing man, Leach said, "Rynning, head out to Blue Buck Canyon. Take the sorrel. See if you can find Crawford."

That night, Leach met with the Comanchero, Sosthenes Archiveque, with Mad Tom looking on. As Cullen Leach began laying out his plan to Archiveque, the leer on the Comanchero's face grew wider. "Any gold you find," Leach said, "is yours to keep."

Archiveque leered evilly.

Chapter Six

George Buckalew cackled as he watched Josh run his hands over the mule's neck. "You surprised me again, son. I never figured you could get them knot-heads back in harness so fast."

Tiny laughed. "Mules are smart, Mr. Buckalew. Smarter than horses. They don't forget."

"That's right," Josh whispered, still caressing the shiny skin on the mule's neck. "They just want you to think they forgot."

Within a few days, the mules were ready. Josh harnessed two of the larger mules as wheelers, the first span next to the freight wagon. The smarter of the two, he harnessed as the near wheeler on the left, and the second as the off wheeler.

53

The smaller mules he planned to use as leaders, but to his dismay, the mule he wanted to use as the near leader refused to respond to the jerk-line commands. Josh muttered a soft curse, "This one has as many brains as a turtle has feathers."

Rolling up his sleeves, revealing his muscular forearms, Tiny grunted. "What about the other one?"

Shaking his head, Josh blew through his lips. "He'll have to do. He's a little hardheaded, but at least he understands the difference between one tug and two tugs."

With a mischievous grin, Tiny glanced up from coupling the second wagon to the first. "I reckon that means you drive."

Josh rolled his eyes.

Tiny feigned regret. "Too bad. I really wanted to handle the ribbons on the wagon, partner, but when it comes to jerk-lines, especially for eight spans, you got me whipped good and proper. I figure if we use eight spans of mules, we can haul close to five thousand pounds."

Josh glared at his partner, muttering one profanity after another.

By lantern light next morning, Josh and Tiny put the mules in harness and backed them up to the lead wagon. He threw his center-fire saddle on the near wheeler while Frenchy and Tiny hooked the chains to the singletrees and ran the jerk-line from the left bit of the near leader to the saddle of the near wheeler.

Josh swung into the saddle on the near wheeler while Tiny, with a grin the size of the Mississippi River, tied his partner's dun to the tailgate of the trailing wagon and rode forward.

"Remember what I told you," said Frenchy, looking up at the two cowpokes. "The trail's clear marked. From here, you hit Little Blue Stage Station. A couple days later, you'll run into the Zulu Stockade. Then—"

Josh interrupted, a grin on his face. He nodded to her husband. "Then we hit the Jones-Plummer Trail. Don't worry, Missus Frenchy. George there burned those directions into our brains."

She laughed and slapped the palm of her hand with her quirt. "One other thing. Back south of here is one of our best customers, the Gaston Ranch. Their sister, Marylee Gaston, is due in from St. Louis. Her brothers came by last night. They want her to take the stage should you run into her. Stage will make it down here in two or three days."

Tiny nodded. "We'll remember."

"And one other thing," the older woman said, her tone filled with caution. "Comancheros and Comanche like to watch the trail. They're all bad, but the worst is a half-Comanche, half-Mexican heathen by the name of Sosthenes Archiveque. You run into him, shoot first."

With Frenchy's warning casting a wide loop in their thoughts, Josh and Tiny pushed out for their first stop, Little Blue Stage Station, just below the caprock, a hard day's journey, especially breaking in a team of sixteen mules that until up to a few days earlier, had been enjoying the freedom of the wild.

For a man his size, Tiny forked his blood bay like a puff of smoke, light in the saddle, anticipating his pony's every move. Throughout the first day, he rode beside the near leader just in case the inexperienced mule missed one of the leads from Josh astride the near wheeler, seven spans of mules back.

With a jerk-line, one mule—the near leader—guides the team. One jerk on the leather ribbon, and the mule moves left, two jerks, right.

Pulling up in a grassy bower for a noon break, Josh set the wagon brake and wrapped the jerk-line around the brake handle, leaving enough slack for the near leader to graze while he and Tiny squatted in the shade of the wagon.

"That leader mule yonder catches on faster than a deacon taking up collection," Josh observed. "You didn't have to do much with him, huh?"

Tiny shoved his battered Stetson to the back of his head. The hot wind stirred his sandy hair as he sipped a tin cup of six-shooter coffee and tore off a piece of jerky. "Not much at all. He followed all your leads. Hard to believe that one's been running wild the last four or five years."

With a chuckle, Josh drained his coffee and nodded to the near leader. "Well, partner, I think you and me got us our Ulysses."

Their eyes constantly scanning the countryside for Comanche and Comanchero, they made good time, reaching Little Blue Stage Station at sunset. They pulled out before sunrise and climbed the caprock to the Staked Plains, thousands of square miles of treeless plains baked hard by the blistering sun, and so named by the Spanish explorers who drove stakes into the plains as a means of finding their way back to camp.

They pulled into Zulu Stockade just after dark. The stockade consisted of two adobes surrounded on all sides by a six-foot adobe wall.

Leaving well before sunrise once again, they continued across the Staked Plains, and soon fell into a hot, dusty routine filled with tedium. Pull out before sunrise, noon, then plod across a tableland fried to a crisp by an unrelenting sun until dark, and then start all over next morning.

The next night, they camped at Chiquita Creek on the border of Indian Territory where they bathed in the cool waters of the creek, oblivious to the fact their mules were bathing right alongside of them.

The days ran together, filled with the constant clamor of clattering chains, jangling O-rings, rattling wagons, all of which were smothered with suffocating heat and choking dust, and blistered by a blinding sun.

After nighting at Beaver in Indian Territory, they headed on to Hine's Crossing where they took the ferry across the Cimarron River. Josh noted the hardcases hanging around the shack. This, he told himself, was a spot to approach with vigilance on the return trip.

Finally, they pulled up in front of the Atchinson, Topeka, and Santa Fe Railroad Station at the end of Front Street in Dodge City, a day early and eager for a hot bath and a good night's sleep.

The baggage clerk indicated two stacks of goods covered with heavy canvas at the end of the loading dock. "Been waiting a week. Didn't know if you old boys going to make it or not. Run into any trouble?"

"Nope," Tiny replied, shifting around in his saddle.

Josh glanced at the setting sun. "Where can we stable our animals for the night? We'll load up in the morning."

After pointing them to the nearest livery, the clerk nodded to a small storage building at the end of the dock. "There be two cases of dynamite in that shed that goes with you. Don't forget it."

Thirty minutes later at the Cattleman's Hotel, Josh leaned back in a bathtub filled with hot water. He sighed wearily. "I could lie here all night," he muttered.

Tiny, his eyes closed, just grunted.

Decked out in a fresh change of clothes, they ambled down the stairs to the dining room where they proceeded to put themselves around a thick steak, cooked just long enough so it wouldn't walk off the plate, fried potatoes, and homemade rolls soaked with butter. To wash it all down, they sipped at a bottle of Old Crow Whiskey.

"So far, so good," Tiny mumbled around a mouthful of grub.

Before Josh could reply, a voice interrupted them. "You the muleskinners for the Buckalew line?"

Josh looked up and stared into a sheriff's badge.

He raised his gaze to a pair of cold eyes and a hard face sporting a handlebar mustache. "Reckon so, Sheriff. Any trouble?"

"Marshal. Not Sheriff." The lanky lawman tapped a slender finger against the badge.

"Sorry, Marshal," Josh replied, noting the well-oiled revolver riding low on the lawman's hip. "What can I do for you?"

The sheriff hooked his thumb over his shoulder. "There's a young lady upstairs been waiting for you boys. Miss Marylee Gaston. I told her I'd send you old boys up to see her if I ran across you. She's in room two-fourteen."

Josh grinned amicably. "We was told she was going to be here. Much obliged for you telling us where we could find her, Marshal." Josh gestured to an empty chair. "Care to sit for a drink?"

With a shrug, the marshal pulled out a chair. "Might as well. Things are quiet right now."

Josh extended his hand. "Name's Josh Carson."

"Mine's Earp. Wyatt Earp."

Tiny looked up from his steak, his eyes wide with disbelief.

"And this here's my partner, Tiny."

A wry grin parted the marshal's thin lips under the handlebar mustache. "Tiny?" He eyed Tiny's massive shoulders and broad chest before sticking his hand in the hamlike clutch of the grinning cowpoke. "This ain't no joke, is it?"

Before Josh could reply, a small man wearing striped pants and a buttoned vest over a boiled shirt scurried up. "Marshal Earp. There's trouble down at the Long Branch Saloon. Sheriff Masterson sent me for you."

Pushing away from the table, Earp touched his fingers to the flat brim of his hat. "Obliged for the offer, boys. Maybe later." He turned on his heel and strode purposely from the dining room.

"Wyatt Earp," muttered Tiny around a mouthful of grub. "I've heard about him, but never reckoned on meeting him."

Josh shook his head. "Me neither." He pointed his fork at Tiny's plate. "When we finish, let's go up and see what Miss Gaston has on her mind."

Tiny only nodded, intent on filling his mouth with steak and potatoes.

Thirty minutes later, they stopped in front of room two-fourteen. Josh knocked.

No answer.

Josh glanced up at Tiny. "Maybe she's out."

Tiny shrugged. "Try again."

At that moment, the door swung open and a slender woman in a high-necked princess dress stared up at them. Her dark hair fell in ringlets on her shoulders, and Josh couldn't help noticing the dimples in her cheeks.

She eyed them with disdain. "Yes?"

Hat in hand, Josh said. "Miss Gaston?"

The slight woman tilted her chin. "Yes."

Josh shifted nervously on his feet. "My name's Josh Carson. This here is my partner, Tiny Hamilton. We're the muleskinners for Buckalew Freight out of Atascocita." He paused, expecting some response, but she simply stared at them.

"We're hauling a load of goods back to Atascocita for the Gaston Ranch. We was told to look you up."

Her face lit with understanding. Her words were sharp and crisp, almost testy. "Oh, yes, now I know who you are. You're here to haul my brothers' shipment back to Atascocita. I saw it on the dock when I arrived. That's how I knew you or someone like you was coming. Is that right?" Before he could reply, she continued, "Well, I'm glad you finally made it. I've been waiting a week. What took you so long?"

Josh parted his lips to reply, but she didn't give him a chance to speak. "Never mind. You're here. That's all that matters. When do you plan on us moving out?"

Taken aback by the torrent of words cascading from her lips, Josh hesitated. "Well, ma'am, we planned on—" Suddenly, his reply stuck in his throat. "Us?" He shook his head and grinned at Tiny. "I must've misunderstood you, ma'am. We, Tiny here and me, we plan on pulling out tomorrow as soon as we load up."

She shook her head and blithely replied, "Oh, no, Mr. Carson. You didn't misunderstand me. I did say *us*. I plan on riding back with you and the goods."

Chapter Seven

Josh sputtered, "But, but, ma'am. That—that just won't work. Besides, your brothers come in and said they want you to ride the stage. That way, you'll be in Atascocita in three days. These old freight wagons take two weeks, and it's hot and slow . . . and those mules, well, ma'am, they smell something fierce."

Her slender jaw set, Marylee Gaston stamped her small foot. "I don't care what John or Matthew said. I have trunks full of belongings that I don't trust anyone to look after except me. I'm riding on the wagons, and that's final."

Josh and Tiny exchanged helpless looks. Tiny cleared his throat. "Please, ma'am. I—"

Her eyes blazed. "I am not a ma'am, I'll have you

64

to know. I am a miss, and that's how I expect to be addressed."

Tiny's square face turned crimson. "Sorry, Miss. But what I was going to say was that Josh and me here, we'll take fine care of your belongings. But, I ain't lying. You truly don't want to spend two weeks bouncing around on them freight wagons."

Josh chimed in. "Tiny's right, Miss Marylee. Besides, we got to face wild heathen Comanches and bloodthirsty Comancheros. The truth is, you'd be a heap safer on the stagecoach."

She jammed her fists into her hips and glared up at the two cowpokes. "My mind is made up, and that's final. I'm going back to Atascocita with you."

Outside the hotel, Josh and Tiny paused on the boardwalk. Josh looked back inside and shook his head. "Now I know how it feels to get run over by a stampede."

Tiny nodded slowly. "Yeah."

Josh drew a deep breath and released it slowly. "Now what? We can't let her go with us. It's too dangerous, and besides, I don't hanker to put up with a female like that."

Tiny removed his hat and scratched his head. "I figure we ought to send one of them telegraphs to Atascocita. Ask what we should do."

Josh shook his head wearily. "There isn't a telegraph in Atascocita."

Grimacing, Tiny blew out through his lips. "Then what do you reckon we ought to do?"

Before he could answer, Wyatt Earp came up. "Howdy, boys. You see the little lady?" There was a smirk on his face that Josh couldn't miss.

"Reckon so, Marshal. As much as I wish we hadn't."

Earp chuckled. "You couldn't talk her out of it, I see."

Tiny blinked once or twice. "You knew what she had on her mind?"

Stroking his mustache, the marshal nodded. "She mentioned it. I tried to talk her out of it, if it's any consolation to you boys."

"Then you know what kind of trouble she's asking for, Marshal. Can't you talk to her again?"

He pulled a black cigar from the inside coat pocket and bit off the end. After touching a lucifer to it, he blew out a stream of smoke and shook his head. "Boys, I make it a point never to try to talk a woman out of anything once she's made up her mind."

"But—"

Earp nodded to Josh. "I know just how dangerous it is, but there's no way you can stop some women from doing what they got their minds set on."

"So, we got to take her. Is that what you're saying, Marshal?"

"I ain't saying nothing," Earp replied. "All I can say is that you boys best keep your eyes open and your six-guns oiled and ready."

Resigned to their fate, Josh and Tiny loaded the two wagons the next morning, but instead of moving out at noon, they spent the afternoon rigging the trailing wagon with sturdy oak bows and covering them with Onasburg canvas, two layers of heavy duck sheets, to provide some protection from the blistering sun and the pounding rain for their unexpected passenger.

As an afterthought, they bought a gentle sorrel mare from the local livery for Marylee just in case she decided she wanted to ride in the saddle instead of on the wagon.

Tiny shook his head. "Miss Marylee is sure causing us a heap of unnecessary trouble, Josh. You know that?"

Josh tied the mare in the livery. He shook his head. "You're not telling me something I don't know."

"I'll tell you what we should've done. We should've loaded up last night and left her behind. Then she would have had to take the stage."

With a rueful grin, Josh grunted. "Now you tell me. Why didn't you say something last night?"

Tiny shrugged. "At least we're all loaded up. We got all of Miss Marylee's plunder loaded on the trailing wagon. So now, all we got to do in the morning is harness the mules and pull out."

Josh finished graining the mare. He shook his head. "I figure we need a drink. How about it?"

Tiny shook his head. "Naw. I'm hungry. You go ahead. I'll get a steak and be on down later."

Five minutes later, Josh bellied up to the silver-trimmed bar at the Long Branch Saloon, Dodge City's finest. After a couple drinks, he looked around the smoky room. In one corner of the elaborately furnished room was the faro table. A few feet beyond was the craps table, and then the roulette.

Several poker games were going on, so Josh sidled over as an uninterested observer, remembering his promise.

An hour later, Tiny lumbered into the Long Branch. He paused at the swinging batwing doors and surveyed the room for Josh. He glimpsed a hand waving in the air at one of the poker tables. Peering through the smoke, the large man's eyes grew wide when he spotted Josh at the table, his hand filled with cards.

Suppressing his anger, Tiny strode over to the

table, ready to yank Josh from the chair and kick his back end all the way out the batwing doors. So much for his promises. But when he reached the table, he jerked to a halt.

On the table in front of Josh was a stack of greenbacks three inches high. Josh glanced up at Tiny and winked, at the same time slapping his cards on the table. "Here you are, boys. Kings over tens."

Cursing, the other three players slammed their cards on the table and glared at Josh as he dragged the pot. One of the players appeared to be a local businessman, but the other two were bearded cowpokes who smelled of trouble.

While the dealer shuffled the cards, one of the cowpokes growled. "You sure are a lucky cuss, cowboy." His eyes narrowed in suspicion.

Josh chuckled. "Just a run of luck, boys. You know what they say about luck. The only thing for sure about it is that sooner or later, it's going to change."

"Well, it sure can't change anytime too soon for me," said the second cowpoke.

"Maybe now's the time," Josh replied as the dealer dealt another hand to the four men. Josh grinned up at Tiny. "Hey, partner. You get enough to eat?"

Before Tiny could answer, the first grizzled cowpoke looked up. "You know this jasper here, cowboy?" he asked in a gravelly voice, nodding to Josh.

Tiny shrugged his massive shoulders. "Yeah. Why?"

The cowpoke's face grew hard. "You go stand behind him. I don't like nobody standing at my back, especially when his partner has got hisself on a big winning streak. Might make a jasper start wondering," he added.

Tiny held him temper and edged around the table to stand behind Josh. He folded his arms across his barrel chest and glared at the cowpoke across the table.

At the same time, Josh dropped his hand to his Colt and slipped the rawhide loop off the hammer. He had a feeling he was playing with a bad loser.

The game rocked back and forth for a few minutes, the pots small, and being fairly distributed among the players.

And then the pot began to grow, each player raising the one before him. By the time the dealer tossed Josh his fifth card, the pot was over a hundred dollars.

Tiny did his best to show no emotion as Josh picked up his last card, the ten of spades, which he neatly slipped into the straight flush, ten high.

Quietly, Josh closed his cards and laid them face down on the table in front of him. He called the bet. When the dealer asked for cards, Josh tapped his forefinger on his and replied, "I'll play these."

The businessman folded.

The two hardcases' eyes narrowed.

Watching the two carefully, Josh kept both his hands, fingers spread, on the table, moving them only to call or bump the bet. When the pot reached two hundred and fifty dollars, betting stopped. Still, Josh kept his hands on the table, his face expressionless, his eyes missing nothing.

One of the cowpokes wore a sneering grin. "I think your luck is about to change, cowboy," he said, slapping down two pair—aces and kings.

"Beats me," said his partner, tossing his cards on the table.

The dealer spoke up. "Show your cards, Mister."

Josh glanced at the businessman beside him. "How about turning them over for me, partner." He fixed his eyes coldly on the sneering cowpoke across the table. "I don't want no one claiming I palmed any cards."

The businessman hesitated, but the dealer nodded. "Go ahead, Carl. Turn the cowboy's cards over."

Tiny shifted his feet. The hair on the back of his neck bristled. He had the feeling that trouble was peeking around the corner. He glanced down at Josh's Colt, and saw with relief that his partner had slipped the rawhide loop off the hammer. Obviously Josh had anticipated some trouble from those two hardcases.

The businessman turned up the six and seven of spades, and the sneer on the hardcase's face faded when the eight of spades was turned up. His eyes grew cold when the nine of spades showed its face, and when the businessman flipped over the ten of spades, he jumped up from the table cursing and grabbing for his six-gun.

Chapter Eight

And then the cowpoke froze, his six-shooter still in its holster, gaping in disbelief at the muzzle of the .44 caliber Colt staring him in the face from across the table.

One of the onlookers whistled. "Jiminy, I never even saw that jasper go for his gun."

Josh stood facing the cowboy. "Don't try it, partner. You don't have a chance."

At that moment, a loud voice interrupted them. "Hold it right there, boys! What the Sam Hill is going on?" It was Earp.

Keeping his eyes on the two cowpokes glaring at him from across the table, Josh explained in a soft, level voice. "Bad losers, Marshal. Ask anyone watching the game."

73

"He's right, Marshal Earp," said the dealer. "Why, this jasper here never even touched the cards after I gave them to him. Ain't no way he could have cheated."

"He had to, Marshal," whined one of the cow-pokes. "Nobody's that lucky."

Earp studied the two. "You the Batton brothers, is that right? Joe and Pete?"

"Yessir, Marshal," said Pete. "Joe here's right. That jasper's been winning all night. Ain't no one wins like that unless they chea—" His words froze on his lips as Earp's black eyes grew cold.

Joe stuttered. "Pete, he wasn't talking about you, Marshal. Why—"

"Shut up, Joe," Earp snapped. "You too, Pete." Keeping his eyes on the two, he spoke over his shoulder to Josh. "You got any objection if I search you, cowboy?"

Tiny started to protest, but Josh stayed him. "Help yourself, Marshal. You won't find nothing. Those two there, why, they just never figured out how to play poker. Bluff when they shouldn't, get all excited with a good hand. I don't have your skill with cards, Marshal, but I know enough to watch a man's face and figure out what's on his mind."

Earp chuckled. "Forget it, cowboy." His voice grew hard. "All right, Pete. You and Joe git. You cause any more trouble tonight, and I'll throw you in jail for the next month, you hear?"

With surly expressions on their faces, the Batton brothers grunted and shuffled from the saloon.

The marshal turned back to Josh. "Where you boys staying, the Cattlemen's Hotel?"

While Josh gathered his winnings and tipped the dealer, Tiny replied, "Yep."

"Well, watch out for those two. They're sneaky all the way down to the soles of their boots. They get a chance, they'll come back for that money." Earp pulled out a black cigar. "Were I you old boys, I'd sleep with one eye open tonight."

Josh touched his fingers to the brim of his Stetson. "Obliged, Marshal."

After Earp had departed, Josh nodded to the bar. "How about one last shot of whiskey before we roll into our soogans, Tiny. The next two weeks is going to be mighty dry."

Just before they left the bar a few minutes later, Carl, the businessman at their table, hurried back in and came straight to Josh. "Figured you best know. The Batton brothers is hiding out behind the tonsorial parlor across the street."

Josh wandered over to the batwing doors and peered across the dimly lit street at the unpainted clapboard building that was the Dodge City Tonsorial Parlor. Next to the tonsorial parlor was a millinery shop, and next to that was the livery where they had stabled their mules and parked the wagons. He turned back with a grin. "Appreciate the information." He nodded to the rear door. "Let's us take the back way to the hotel, Tiny. What do you say?"

Tiny grinned and downed the rest of his whiskey.

Before lighting the lamp in their room, Josh squinted out the window facing Front Street. Candle lamps lit the street like dull yellow balloons. "Wonder how long those old boys plan on hunkering down behind the tonsorial parlor," he muttered.

Tiny chuckled. "They'd best not use the barber's outhouse is all I can say. I went over for a haircut before supper. I had to go to his outhouse. It was a three holer, but there was a big hornet's nest inside."

Josh chuckled. "So what did you do?"

"Don't ask. Hey, there's one of them brothers now."

Sure enough, Pete eased far enough from the building to step in the glow of the dim light from the streetlamp.

Keeping his eyes on Pete, Tiny said, "So, what are we going to do?"

Josh pondered the question several moments. "I never cared much to wait around and let trouble come to me."

With a rueful grin, Tiny remembered the times Josh had forced issues just so he wouldn't have to worry about them. "What you got in mind?"

Stroking his jaw and staring at Pete Batton, he said, "Tell you what." He turned and grinned up at his partner. "With those two skulking around down there, we're not going to get any sleep tonight anyway, so let's us pack our soogans. You get Miss Marylee. I'll take care of those two jaspers down there, and we'll move out tonight. There's a full moon. We can make fifteen, maybe twenty miles before the sun comes up."

Lifting a skeptical eyebrow, Tiny shook his head. "They'll follow us, Josh. You know as sure as hogs wallowing in mud, they'll be bound to follow us."

With a soft chuckle, Josh made a sweeping gesture of the town. "At least, it'll be on our ground, not on theirs." He grabbed his soogan and started packing it with his plunder. "I'll take care of those two. You get Miss Marylee down to the livery in fifteen minutes. That's when we're moving out."

Tiny looked up from packing his gear. "Me? What if she don't want to go?"

With a wicked chuckle, Josh replied, "Tell her to catch the next stage. That'll get her going."

Josh eased down the back stairs and headed down the alley. At the end of the block, he slipped up the side of Grogan's General Store and dropped to his knees at the corner, studying Front Street, waiting for the right opportunity to dash across the street.

A few minutes later, the opportunity arose when gunfire broke out down at the Long Branch. Without hesitation, Josh dropped into a crouch and raced across the street, disappearing into the shadows of the livery.

In the darkness, he made out the outline of his loaded wagons. He glanced in the direction of the tonsorial parlor. First, he had to take care of the Batton brothers. He remembered the outhouse Tiny had told him about, and a devious plan exploded in his head.

Silently, he slipped through the darkness, a roll of binding twine in his pocket and a well-used, limber rope over his shoulder. He paused at the rear of the millinery shop, crouching in the shadows.

Moments later, Pete materialized from the darkness. Josh searched the murky shadows for Joe, and then heard the brother's voice from the front of the tonsorial parlor. "You back there?"

Pete whispered, "Yeah. See anything?"

"Nothing."

"Wonder when them jaspers is coming out?"

Joe growled. "Be quiet back there."

Pete was already quiet by that time for Josh had

laid the butt of his Colt across the brother's temple. Quickly, he bound and gagged the unconscious *hombre*, then dragged him into the outhouse and propped him up on one of the three holes.

Just as Josh started to push open the door, Joe called out, "You in there again, Pete. I swear, I don't know what I'm going to do with y—" He opened the door and Josh whopped him good and solid on the forehead.

Quickly hogtying Joe, Josh placed him on the adjoining hole to Pete, and then using the binding twine, gingerly looped it around the neck of the hornet's nest and tied the other end to the back of Joe's gunbelt.

Minutes later, Josh was back in the livery and had the mules in harness. He had just finished hooking up the wheelers' trace chains to the singletrees when the barn door banged open and Marylee Gaston stormed in with Tiny, loaded down with the irate woman's luggage, right behind her.

She jerked to a halt when she saw Josh. "Just what are you doing? I'll have you fired for this, you—you—" She shook her head. "Whoever heard of leaving at such an hour?"

Josh attempted to explain. "Look, Miss Marylee. We don't have time to explain it all right now. Just climb up in the second wagon, and I'll explain later. Right now, we need to pull out."

She stamped her foot. "I am not going anywhere at this time of the night, and not even that—that—" She jabbed a finger at Tiny who was loading her luggage in the wagon. "And not even that overgrown bull can make me." She set her jaw and glared at Josh.

"If that's how you want it then. You can just catch the next stage out."

"No! I'm not going anywhere, and you're not going anywhere."

Tiny shrugged and gave Josh a helpless look.

Josh nodded once or twice, then gestured for Tiny to deposit Marylee Gaston in the second wagon.

The surprised young woman screamed when Tiny seized her by her slender waist and promptly set her on the second wagon.

At that moment, a voice boomed from the doorway. "What the Sam Hill is going on in here?"

Josh looked around. The imposing figure standing in the doorway was Marshal Earp. He came toward them, stopping in front of the team of mules.

His arms still outstretched overhead, Tiny looked around and froze.

Earp sauntered up to the trailing wagon, his eyes narrowed. "Well, now, muleskinners. What's going on here?"

"We're pulling out, Marshal. Miss Marylee wants us to wait until tomorrow. That's why she's pitching such a fit." Josh glanced at the slight woman who was glaring pitchforks at him.

She tilted her chin and looked down at the marshal from where she was perched on the wagon. "Marshal Earp, I demand you keep these wagons here until I am ready to leave."

Earp arched an eyebrow. "Demand?" He grunted. "And just who might you be, Missy, to demand anything around here?"

Before she could reply, Josh said, "She's a spoiled brat from a rich family back in Atascocita who wants her to take the stage. But she decided that since Tiny and me are too ignorant to look after her belongings on the wagons, she's got to go along with us."

A slow grin drifted across the Marshal's face. "Well, then, Miss, I suggest you either take the stage, or stay up there on the wagon where you are and keep those pretty lips shut."

Marylee turned her fiery glare from Josh back to the marshal but remained in the wagon. "I—I'll have your job for this. Why—"

Ignoring her, Earp spoke to Josh. "I haven't seen the Batton boys around the last hour or so, and their horses are still at the hitching rail in front of the Long Branch. You didn't kill them, did you? Not that it would bother me, but it would cause me a heap of paperwork."

Josh grinned. "Got them tied up good and proper in the outhouse behind the tonsorial parlor, Marshal. They're not hurt none."

Marshal Earp bit the tip off a cigar and lit it. "It still got that big hornet's nest in it?"

The picture of innocence, Josh shrugged. "Why, I never paid any attention to a hornet's nest, Marshal. I just figured it was a snug place to keep them out of our hair until we could get out of Dodge."

Earp laughed and stepped aside. "Well, then, I reckon if you're going, you'd best move out. Of course, you know," he added as the wagons rattled past him, "them Batton brothers will be coming after you."

Chapter Nine

The prairie night was cool and the stars overhead shone like a field full of fireflies. The only sounds of the night were the soft thud of hooves cutting into the dry soil and the rattling of trace chains.

Josh glanced over his shoulder at the trailing wagon where Marylee was sleeping and shook his head. He wasn't looking forward to the next several days.

Tiny rode some distance ahead, like Josh, his eyes constantly quartering the darkness and his ears tuned to any stray noise that didn't belong.

Back in Dodge City, Pete Batton jerked awake, the stench of the outhouse burning his nose. He tried to move his arms, but unlike his feet, they were tied. He felt someone next to him. "Joe? That you?"

His brother moaned. "What happened? All I remember is I opened the outhouse door, and then everything went blank."

"Your hands tied?"

"Huh?" Suddenly Joe broke into a string of cursing. "What's going on here?" He jumped to his feet and twisted around, pulling the binding twice as taut and yanking the hornet's nest from the corner of the ceiling. "Who in the Sam Hill—" He screamed as the first hornet hit him. "Out, out, out," he shouted, running over his brother in a frantic effort to get out the door.

Pete bounced against the wall and fell back under Joe's feet, sending them both spilling halfway out the open door and onto the ground, perfect targets for the infuriated hornets.

Lights popped on around town as their screams carried down Front Street and up the alleyways.

Finally stumbling to their feet as the hornets besieged them, the two brothers took off running, arms still bound at their sides. Pete glanced over his shoulder, and then when he looked around, he ran into the corner of the tonsorial parlor, knocking himself to the ground unconscious.

Joe made it to the street. The last the town saw of him that night, he was racing across the prairie with the hornets in hot pursuit.

* * *

The remainder of the night passed quickly for Josh and Tiny, and as the sun crept over the eastern horizon, the two cowpokes began looking over their back trail toward Dodge City. Tiny rode up and nodded to the trailing wagon. "Reckon we best give our passenger some grub and water," he said, fishing out some dry biscuits and jerky. "It'll be a few hours before we noon."

Josh, astride the near wheeler, nodded and pulled out a bag of Bull Durham. While he built a cigarette, he studied the prairie around them. Flat and dry. One mile was like the next under the blistering sun. Not much different than the Staked Plains down in Texas.

"We ought to make Brown's Soddy by tomorrow night," Josh muttered when Tiny returned. "How's she doing?"

Tiny grinned. "I got the feeling she's having second thoughts."

"Too late now," Josh said, taking a drag off the cigarette. "She'll just have to tough it out."

Four hours later, Josh reined up the team in the best graze he could find. While Tiny put on the coffee, he used his hat to water the mules.

Marylee, a thin layer of fine dust covering her high-necked dress and cinched-in waist, stormed up. "Why did you stop here? There's no shade." She dabbed at her forehead with a lacy handkerchief.

"I'm hot and sweaty. At least when we were moving, there was a breeze."

Watering the last mule, Josh nodded. "Best graze around, Miss Marylee. For the mules. They need to eat and rest a bit. Besides, you take a look, you'll see there's no shade to be seen. Won't be any until we hit Brown's Soddy tomorrow afternoon."

Tiny handed her a cup. "Coffee, Miss Marylee?"

She took the cup and looked around. "What about bathing? I didn't see any tub on the wagon."

Josh kept his eyes on the small fire so she wouldn't see the laughter in them. "Don't have any, Miss. The only time we get a bath on the trail is if it rains or we cross a river."

The young woman just stared at them, unable to believe her ears. "You mean—"

"Yes, ma'am," Josh replied.

"But—I—" Her words died in her slender throat as a tiny frown wrinkled her forehead and tears glistened in her eyes. Her lips quivered.

Tiny tried to reassure her. "It ain't that bad, Miss Marylee. Honest." He cleared his throat and then in an apologetic tone, continued, "I don't mean to offend you, but if you don't mind me saying so, you'd be a heap more comfortable in some duds that fit looser. That way the air can circulate around your—" He hesitated, a crimson blush running up his thick neck and covering his square face. He gestured futilely at her slender frame. "Well, you know."

Marylee drew a deep breath and patted the ringlets dangling about her shoulders. She stood a little more erect. "I'll have you know that proper ladies don't wear loose clothes like that, not in today's world." And with that, she turned on her heel and stomped back to her wagon.

His eyes on her, Tiny muttered, "You think I need to help her up on the wagon, Josh?"

The slender cowpoke shoved his hat to the back of his head and studied her back. "I don't reckon so. I guess she can make it herself, after all she just told us that she knows what proper ladies are supposed to do in today's world. You and me, Tiny, we're just ignorant muleskinners."

Finally, after several unsuccessful attempts, Marylee managed to climb up on her perch in the wagon.

Back in Atascocita, Big Nose Cartwright, followed by Dave Rynning and Mad Tom Gristy, stopped in front of Cullen Leach's desk. "You wanted us, Mr. Leach?"

Leach leaned back in his swivel chair and stuck his thumbs in his vest. He studied Rynning and Gristy a few moments, then waved them away. "I'm not going to need you boys. I want to save you for later. This is between me and Cartwright here."

After the two left, Cartwright frowned down at Leach. "I don't understand, Mr. Leach."

Leach leaned forward and extracted a cigar from the humidor on his desk. With a pair of cigar clips, he snipped off the end of the cigar and touched a match to it. After blowing out a stream of smoke, he cleared his throat. "I figure the wagons are pulling out of Dodge City about now. It'll be at least another week before they reach Little Blue Stage Station. I want you to pick up three or four gunnies—ones not known around here. Be waiting for those wagons when they come off the caprock."

Big Nose frowned, puzzled. "But, Mr. Leach. Where can I find *hombres* like that? They ain't no new faces in Atascocita."

Shaking his head, the balding man snorted. "I didn't figure on you finding them here. Get over to Hidetown. You'll find them there."

Big Nose's craggy face lit in understanding. "All right, Mr. Leach. I see what you want. Do you want me to bring them back here?"

Leach snorted and slammed his fat hand down on the desk. "No, I don't want them back here. I don't want anyone to know they're working for me, understand? And when you get the wagons, take them out to my ranch. Go the back way, around town. I'll come out and pay them off, fifty dollars each." He dipped his head toward Crawford. "Do you understand now? Are you sure you understand?"

Crawford grinned wickedly. "Yes, sir. I understand. I understand real good."

At dusk, the freight wagons pulled up at the base of a slight rise. As the gray of dusk gave way to the dark of night, from horizon to horizon stars started popping out thicker than cloves on a Christmas ham.

Josh pulled the wagons into an L shape, then hung a canvas fly overhead while Tiny draped canvas from the sideboards to the ground to hide the blaze of the small fire.

While Tiny put a pot of jerky stew on to simmer along with a pot of six-shooter coffee, Josh tended the mules, watering them, checking their hooves, and then cross-hobbling them. They were in good shape. He grinned. Frenchy sure had herself some fine mules here.

As he headed back to the shelter, a roll of thunder

reverberated from the south. He glanced in that direction to see a lightning-laced bank of storm clouds rolling toward them, obliterating the stars.

He ducked under the canvas fly into the crude shelter. Before he could pour a cup of coffee, Marylee called out to him from her wagon. "Oh, Mr. Carson. If you don't mind, I'll have my dinner in here tonight."

Josh bit his tongue. After all, he told himself, what can you expect from a greener who had no idea what the west was like. He blew out through his lips. "Yes, ma'am. I'll bring it over." He couldn't help chuckling. Sooner or later, she'd learn the truth.

By the time he delivered her bowl of stew, dried biscuits, and steaming coffee, the storm was within minutes of striking. The air crackled with electricity.

She eyed the supper. "What is this?"

"Why, jerky stew and biscuits, Miss. That's what we have on the trail."

She dumped the bowl of stew and biscuits on the ground. "No, thank you. I'm not hungry."

Josh suppressed his retort. "Whatever you say, Miss Marylee." Before she could retreat back into her wagon, Josh pointed out the clouds. "Looks like we're in for a real gully washer. You might want to come over to the tent."

She sniffed. "No, thank you. I'll be just fine in here," she replied, gesturing to the thick duck canvas over her head.

Josh stepped back down off the wagon wheel on which he was standing. "Whatever you say, Miss. We'll be over there if you should need something."

"I won't. Thank you." She snorted imperiously.

Chapter Ten

The storm hit with a vengeance, thunder booming, lightning cracking and popping, sending blazing trunks of fire hurtling at the ground, bursting in ear-splitting explosions. Rain pounded down in sheets.

Josh had slanted the overhead canvas at an angle so the water would run off. The canvas sides popped in and out with the gusts of rain, but Tiny had staked them securely so that inside the small shelter, they were snug and warm.

Josh leaned back on his saddle and sipped at his cup of six-shooter coffee. "You made it good tonight, partner," he said, pulling out his bag of Bull Durham. "Your coffee is thicker than molasses. I reckon it would float a horseshoe." He laughed and took another swallow of the coffee.

Tiny cut his eyes in the direction of the trailing wagon. "What about her, Josh? She's got to be scared with all this lightning and thunder."

"I asked her to come over here," he replied, not wanting Tiny to know just how worried he was about Marylee Gaston. "But she knows everything. Let her find out for herself." He hoped Tiny would protest. That would give him a reason to try to persuade her once again to share their snug shelter.

To his dismay, Tiny shrugged and lay back on his saddle and stretched his long legs, crossing his feet with the soles of his boots facing the small, but warm fire. "If you say so."

Before Josh could reply, a shrill shriek cut through the roar of the storm. The two cowpokes leaped to their feet and dashed from the canvas shelter. A bolt of chain lightning exploded, illuminating the night with a ghostly white light.

Marylee was sitting on her derriere in the middle of a mud puddle, staring in disbelief at her hands, which were covered with mud. Josh suppressed a grin as they hurried to her, each lifting her gently by her arms and helping her to the tent. "Easy, Miss," said Tiny. "This mud is slicker than calf slobber."

Josh bit his tongue to keep from laughing.

Once inside, the bedraggled woman jerked from their hands and threw her shoulders back. She wiped her muddy hands on her dress and then squeezed out the water cascading down her hair, straightening her ringlets. Her blue dress sagged on her slender frame, and the makeup she had so painstakingly painted on her face ran in dark streaks down her cheeks.

She looked at Josh and Tiny with as much dignity as she could muster, then, trying to control her shivering, said, "I decided I would take your offer of waiting out the storm in here."

Josh tried to appear sympathetic as he looked upon the disheveled figure before him. She would run a wet cat a close race for the most weather-beaten creature around.

"Here you are, Miss Marylee. Take a seat right here," said Josh, indicating his soogan. "I reckon some hot coffee would hit the spot about now."

Tiny grabbed a blanket. "I reckon this might help you ward off any chills, Miss Marylee," he said, draping the blanket about her slender shoulders. He nodded to the spider of jerky stew bubbling over the fire. "We got plenty to eat, Miss, if you might be hungry."

After drying her face with a corner of the blanket, Marylee sipped the coffee. "This will do fine, thank you very much," she replied in a stiff voice.

"I don't know, Miss Marylee," Josh said. "Rain and weather like this, a body needs nourishment, something to keep it warm. You might not be hungry, but it wouldn't hurt to be on the safe side."

She eyed the bubbling pot eagerly. "Well, maybe just a small bowl."

She ate three bowls before she dropped off to sleep, curled in Josh's soogan and resting her head on his saddle. Outside, the storm battered at the small shelter.

The next morning when Marylee Gaston peeked out of the tent, Josh was removing the cross-hobbles from the mules, and Tiny had just finished dishing up a heap of fried bacon and a stack of thin johnnycakes in a tin plate. He grinned at her. "Morning, Miss. Coffee's hot and breakfast is ready." He folded a johnnycake around a couple slices of bacon and dipped it in the bacon grease remaining in the spider. He smacked his lips. "Ain't nothing better than bacon and johnnycakes."

She stood there a moment staring at him, her hair a tangle of knots, her dress stained and drooping, and her face streaked with makeup. She glanced at Josh who ignored her. "No, thank you. I'm not hungry."

Before Tiny could reply, her stomach growled. He dragged the back of his hand across his lips and gave her an amiable grin. "Well, Miss, maybe you ain't, but it sure sounds to me like your stomach is."

Her face grew hard, then softened into a smile. "You know, Mr. Hamilton, I think you might just be right."

He gestured to a log by the fire. "Then have a seat, Miss. And my name is Tiny. I'll dish you up a plate."

Overhearing the conversation, Josh figured that maybe Marylee Gaston had finally grown up, but later that day when she began whining about the constant bouncing of the wagon, he knew he was wrong.

To his relief, they pulled into Brown's Soddy in Meade County, Kansas, early that afternoon. Maybe Mrs. Klarner, who owned the waystation with her husband, Ben, could keep Marylee Gaston out of his hair for a few hours, Josh told himself.

Another storm rolled in that night. Inside the snug soddy with the rain beating against the wooden shutters covering the windows, Marylee informed Josh and Tiny she was tired of riding in the wagon.

They were sitting at a rough-hewn table downing a supper of bean soup, sourdough bread, and hot coffee. The two cowpokes exchanged a quick glance. "That's just fine, Miss Marylee," Josh said. "We'll saddle the little mare we picked up back in Dodge. "All you need to remember, Miss," he added, warning her, "don't go riding off out of sight. Best you stay close to the wagons. Injuns out there can pop right out of the ground."

She arched a skeptical eyebrow, but remained silent.

Josh rose well before dawn next morning to check the load for water damage and then saddle the mare. He paused outside the door of the soddy and stared at the sky, washed fresh and clean by the storms. He stretched his arms over his head and grinned. It was going to be a good day.

A guttural voice cut into his thought. "That's it, cowboy. Keep them arms stretched high over your head."

He looked around into the sneering grins on the faces of two strangers.

Keeping his eyes on Josh, one spoke to his partner. "This the jasper that won all the money, Shorty?"

Shorty nodded and a cruel grin played over his fat face, revealing half a dozen gaps in his rotting teeth. "Yeah. That's him, Windy."

The tall angular man gestured with the muzzle of his revolver. "Let's have it, cowboy. It sure ain't worth eating a lead biscuit for."

Josh's brain raced. "Reckon you're right about that, partner."

"So, let's have it."

Hesitating momentarily, Josh stepped from in front of the soddy door, hoping that someone would open it and draw their attention long enough for him to shuck his .44 Colt.

"I don't have it," he replied, playing for time.

Shorty's eyes narrowed. "Where is it?" His nervous eyes flicked to the closed door.

"The barn," Josh said, glancing at the wagons in the rawhide and stick-pole barn.

"Let's go," muttered Windy. "The barn. Now."

Josh stared at the rail-thin man.

"You heard me," Windy growled. "Get the money."

Feigning resignation with a long sigh, Josh headed for the barn, still holding his hands over his head and desperately hoping for some distraction that would give him time to react.

Shorty prodded him in the back with the muzzle of his revolver. "And no tricks."

At that moment, Josh's chance came.

"Hey," Tiny shouted from the soddy. "What the Sam Hill is going on out there? Josh! You all right?"

The shout distracted the two owlhoots just long enough for Josh to spin to his left, knocking aside Shorty's six-gun with his left hand, and send a knotted fist crashing into the corpulent jasper's temple.

In reflex, Shorty squeezed the trigger. His revolver

belched flame, and Windy screamed, doubling over in pain and grabbing his right thigh.

At the same time, Josh shucked his own Colt and thumbed back the hammer as Shorty, his pig-eyes blazing with fury, spun back around and lifted his revolver.

Josh fired. The two hundred grain slug caught Shorty in the bend of his elbow, shattering his arm and sending him sprawling to the ground.

Tiny raced up, six-gun in hand. Moments later, led by Marylee Gaston, the Klarners and three of their customers poured from the open door of the soddy, startled by the gunfire.

Mrs. Klarner mended the two owlhoots the best she could, and Josh sent them on their way back to Dodge City with the chilling warning, "Either of you cross me again, you'll never see that first shovel of dirt the undertaker throws in your face."

A few minutes later when they pulled out for Hine's Crossing, Josh blinked several times at Marylee. To his surprise, she had shed her dress and was wearing riding clothes, soft leather boots, a split skirt, and a loose-fitting blouse under a vest. Josh and Tiny exchanged smug looks, but neither said a word.

To Josh's surprise, Marylee followed Josh's instructions, never riding more than forty or fifty yards from the wagons. And to his further surprise, she appeared to be an experienced rider, forking her mare like a man instead of sidesaddle.

As dusk approached, the trees lining the Cimarron River eased into sight. Tiny reined his pony around and waved toward the river. "There's Hine's Crossing."

Josh remembered Hine's Crossing too well. The station was nothing more than a weather-beaten shack on the river's edge with a rope ferry spanning the river. "We'll camp out here," he said, recollecting the hardcases lounging about the station on the ride up.

Marylee reined up. "Why don't we go on in? I'd like to visit with another woman."

Tiny pulled up. "No women there, Miss. Nothing but a bunch of hardcases and scavengers, them that feed off folks like us. Josh is right. We'd best stay out here until morning, and then ride in."

"And when we do," Josh added, patting the butt of his .44 Colt, "we ride in with our eyes open and our guns ready."

They made a cold camp that night. Marylee Gaston slept little, remembering Josh's last words.

Next morning well before sunrise, Josh rolled them out of their bedrolls and headed for the crossing.

Sitting back from the shore forty or fifty yards, the shack appeared deserted although four or five horses milled about in the rawhide and stick corral by the barn out back. Josh glanced at Tiny and nodded to the rifle under the big man's saddle fender. "Keep that Spencer ready."

Tiny winked as Josh drove the wagons up on the ferry that was docked at the shore of the river. Once they were on the ferry and quickly chained down, he called out, "Hello, there. You got customers."

There was no response for a few minutes, but he spotted furtive faces peering from the darkened windows.

"Hello," he shouted again. "Anyone there?"

A lanky jasper who looked more like a scarecrow than a human staggered out the door and almost fell off the porch. "Be right there," he shouted. "Hold your horses, pilgrims." He gestured to the corral. "I gots to see about my animals."

Tiny shot Josh a warning look. Josh whispered urgently to Marylee, "I don't care what happens, stay behind that mare." He nodded to his partner. "Tiny, pull us across. We're not waiting."

With a crooked grin, the big man shrugged his shoulders and wrapped his massive fingers about the tow rope. "Hold on. Here we go."

His muscles bulged, straining the fabric of his

linen shirt, and the ferry surged into the current of the Cimarron River.

At that moment, the lanky jasper came running around the corner of the shack shouting for them to stop, and behind him came four hardcases with six-guns firing in a desperate effort to stop the ferry.

Six-guns are accurate only at a short distance, and the growing distance between the ferry and the shore had the scavengers' slugs humming like a swarm of drunken bees in every direction, occasionally splatting into a wagon or ripping a chunk out of one of the tow posts. Mostly, the leap plums simply erupted geysers in the water around the ferry.

Josh yanked his Winchester from the boot and dropped to one knee as a slug tugged on his vest. The distance to the shore was growing, but with a rifle, it was still like shooting proverbial sitting ducks, so he deliberately tried to knock a leg from one, hit an arm of another, but with all the dodging and jumping around the scavengers were doing, he knew that he had hit a couple jaspers bad, so bad they probably wouldn't see the sun go down that day.

As the ferry reached midstream, the fire from the bank ceased. Two or three of the scavengers limped about. Another two lay motionless on the ground.

Once they reached shore, Josh lost no time in disembarking from the ferry. "We got us another twelve hours of daylight," he shouted, driving the mules from the ferry. "We can make another fifteen or twenty miles before night."

As the wagons clattered ashore, Tiny reined up. "You reckon those jaspers will follow us?"

Josh glanced at Marylee, whose face was pale as snow. "They don't have the stomach for it." He paused, and a look of concern stiffened his slender face. "I'm more worried about the Batton brothers than these jaspers."

Chapter Eleven

At the same time the freight wagons pulled out for Beaver Station in Indian Territory, Big Nose Crawford and four hardcases rode out of Hidetown, two days due east of Atascocita.

He led the small band northwest, planning on cutting the Jones-Plummer trail just below the caprock only a few miles north of Little Blue Stage Station. He glanced over his shoulder at the hardcases he had hired and shivered. He had been around tough *hombres* before. In fact, he considered himself one. He had no qualms about killing, but these four . . . he grimaced. There was something about them that made the hair on the back of his neck bristle.

Still, they could get the job done, and that's what Cullen Leach was paying them for. He laid his hand on the butt of his pearl-handled revolver, drawing comfort in the feel of cold metal against his rugged palm.

The blazing sun washed the blue out of the sky, leaving a white bowl overhead as the solitary wagons clattered over the Jones-Plummer Trail across the panhandle of Indian Territory.

After hours in the saddle, Marylee, her eyes vacant, her shoulders sagging, sat listlessly as her mare plodded beside the wagon. Tiny continued riding point. As far as the eye could see, blue grama struggled with sagebrush for what little moisture the thin soil contained.

Despite the debilitating heat and choking dust, they were making good time. "We should reach Beaver tonight, and Chiquita Creek tomorrow."

Just before dusk, Tiny reined up and waved his Stetson back and forth, then dug his heels into the pony and rode south.

A few minutes later, Marylee rode up. "Where's Tiny going?"

"Waystation up ahead. Beaver. About thirty minutes. He's riding in to make sure there's no problems. If not, then at least you'll have a roof over your head tonight."

"And a bath?" Gingerly she tugged on her sleeve with two fingers.

Before Josh could reply, a slug slammed into the wagon sideboard behind him, followed instantly by the boom of a rifle.

Startled by the shot, the young woman's sorrel reared and pawed at the sky, sending Marylee tumbling to the ground. "Stay down," Josh shouted, shucking his Winchester and leaping from the near wheeler in one motion. The mules bolted, ran a few yards, then pulled up.

Stunned by the sudden commotion, Marylee tried to stagger to her feet, but Josh threw out his arm as he hit the ground, dragging her back down. "Stay down, I said," he shouted, rolling onto his belly and touching off two quick shots.

Two more shots rang out, tearing up chunks of baked earth by his head. They had him quartered. One of the jaspers was to his left, the other straight ahead.

Off to his right, he spotted a buffalo wallow. He grabbed her arm. "Over there. That hollow. When I start shooting, run for it. Ready?"

She gulped, but nodded.

"All right," he shouted, rising to one knee and tossing off two shots in the direction of each of the bushwhackers. Marylee leaped to her feet, racing for the wallow. She stumbled forward, tumbling into the wallow.

He dashed after her, and in the next instant, Josh

sprawled in the dust at her side as slugs hummed over their heads. He rolled onto his back and quickly reloaded the Winchester. He jerked up and snapped off half a dozen shots in the general direction of his attackers.

"Muleskinner!"

Josh recognized the raspy voice of Joe Batton. He remained silent, trying to pinpoint the hardcase's location.

Batton called out once again. "All we want is our money. Give it to us and you can get on your way. And don't figure on no help from that overgrown partner of yours. Pete's watching the trail. You ain't getting no help from nowhere."

On her stomach, Marylee looked around at Josh, her eyes wide. Smudges of dirt stained her cheeks. "What's he talking about? What money?"

Josh ignored her questions. "Can you shoot?"

"What?"

He snapped. "I said, can you shoot?" He held out the Winchester. "Just lever a cartridge in the chamber, pull the trigger, and—"

Her eyes blazed. She grabbed the Winchester and promptly fired off three shots into the air. "Like that?"

A slow grin played over his lips. He took the Winchester and filled the magazine, then handed it back to her. "Here. You have fifteen shots in there. About every minute or two, fire off a couple into the air."

A frown knit her brow. "Where are you going?"

By now, the sun had set and dusk was deepening. "Don't worry." He shook his head and shucked his six-gun. "Give me five minutes, and we'll be on our way." Without another word, Josh rolled over and slipped out of the wallow on his belly, moving from sage to sage in a broad circle around Batton. He didn't figure on worrying about Pete for he was watching the south trail for Tiny.

Josh peered through the sagebrush, trying to spot Batton, but nothing moved in the gray shadows falling over the prairie. Two shots rang out from Marylee, but still Josh saw nothing. Rolling onto his back, he slipped a .44 cartridge from his gunbelt and hurled it at the mules.

The cartridge hit the near leader, Ulysses, on the rump, startling the animal. With a loud braying, the mule jerked the team forward at the same time Marylee fired two more shots.

Peering into the sage, Josh glimpsed movement thirty feet distant as Joe poked his head above the sage to see where the wagons were heading. Grateful for the ever-growing dusk, Josh squirmed over the blue grama, staying below the crown of purple sage until he was directly behind Joe Batton.

He rose to his feet, his jaw set, his dark eyes black as ice. He held his Colt at his side, and in a low voice, said, "Batton!"

Joe Batton stiffened. For several moments, he lay motionless on his belly, then started to turn over.

"Don't turn over with the Winchester in your hand, Batton. You'll never make it."

The prone man tossed the Winchester aside. He muttered a curse. "All right to turn over now?"

"Just be easy."

Batton rolled over and glared at Josh.

The lanky cowpoke raised his six-gun and aimed it at Joe Batton's chest. "I don't want to kill you, Joe, but I will if you don't call your brother in right now."

The grizzled hardcase licked his lips. "What are you going to do to us?"

"You'll see. Now call him in, and tell him to holster that hogleg. I see it in his hand, and you'll be taking that first step down the stairway to Hades."

Reluctantly, the surly cowpoke did as Josh ordered. Moments later, a puzzled and chagrined Pete Batton appeared from the darkness, his six-shooter holstered.

In the distance, the pounding of racing hooves cut through the silence of the night. The stars lit the prairie with a bluish silver glow, and in the distance, Josh made out the silhouette of his partner driving his blood bay at breakneck speed toward them.

Tiny jerked back on the reins, yanking his pony into a sliding halt and leaping to the ground in the same motion. "What the—"

"Nothing to worry about, partner. Just our friends from the poker game back in Dodge. Tried to bushwhack us."

Moments later, Marylee appeared, carrying the Winchester in both hands, ready to jerk it to her shoulder if necessary.

Tiny took a few steps toward the brothers. "Let's take them on to Beaver. Those folks sure don't cotton to bushwhackers. They'll leave these two gargling on a rope."

Marylee gasped.

Josh shook his head, his eyes fixed on the two subdued men. "No. Maybe we should, but these two old boys are so dumb, they can't tell skunks from housecats. Hate to see a jasper hanged for just being dumb." He cocked his .44. "All right, boys. Shed the hoglegs." Without taking his eyes from them, he said, "Tiny, grab their Winchesters."

Her voice trembling with anxiety, Marylee spoke up. "You're not going to shoot them, are you?"

"No," Josh drawled. "I'm sending them back to Dodge."

"Without our guns?" Joe exclaimed. "What about them renegade Kiowas? We'll be scalped."

"You got your knife and your pony. You best spot any Kiowa before he spots you. Now, git!"

"But—" began Pete.

His voice cold and unyielding, Josh cut him off. "You keep jawing, I'll change my mind and take your boots and make you walk."

Joe elbowed his brother. "Shut up, Pete. Let's get our horses and get out of here. We can make forty miles before sunrise. Kiowas and Comanche don't roam much at night." Muttering under his breath, they turned and headed back northeast toward Dodge.

Leaving Beaver before sunrise the next morning, Josh figured they should reach Chiquita Creek about mid-afternoon on the Texas border.

Later that day, he glanced at Marylee who had endured the day stoically despite the swirling dust and the debilitating heat from the blazing sun. She sat her saddle woodenly, her eyes lifeless and her clothes caked with a layer of dust.

Josh cleared his throat. "I was thinking, Miss Marylee, that we should hit Chiquita Creek soon. That might be a good time to take a little break and rest the mules."

His words jerked her from her heat-induced stupor. Her eyes brightened. "Chiquita Creek! A real creek, with clean water?"

A grin split his slender face, which had been considerably darkened by the last several days in the sun. "Clean enough for a body to wash himself up good and proper."

Life came back into her eyes, and an animated smile parted her lips. "That sounds wonderful."

While Tiny built a small fire and put coffee on, Josh watered the mules and picketed them in a patch of lush graze. He then strung up a canvas tarp upstream by a deep pool of clear, cold water to provide the young lady privacy before he joined Tiny downstream, wading in fully dressed except for his boots, vest, and gunbelt.

Pausing as she climbed out of her wagon with an armload of towels and fresh clothing, the young woman frowned at the two cowboys.

When Tiny saw the puzzled expression on her face, he laughed. "Being there's a lady present, Miss, this is the most respectable way we can get our skin and our clothes clean."

She shook her head and clambered down from the wagon. Although she had been gone from Dodge City only a few days, it seemed like months, and Philadelphia seemed like the other side of the world.

* * *

The pool Josh had selected for her was in the bend of the creek that angled to the south for several feet, then cut back to the east, surrounded on both banks by thick plum thickets.

When the two cowpokes saw her disappear into the thicket, they quietly slipped from the water, and spread out so they could see any unwanted visitors long before they neared the thicket, at the same time letting the sun dry their clothes on their backs.

Marylee smiled gratefully when she reached the small clearing on the shore of the stream. With the canvas hung on the perimeter of the clearing, she realized she had all the privacy she could wish for.

The cold water tingled her flesh. She took her time, soaping up several times and ducking into the icy water to rinse.

She swam into the deeper hole in the chilly creek and, turning on her back and staring at the spreading limbs overhead and the wispy clouds beyond, couldn't help feeling a strange kinship with the generations of Indians who perhaps had once lived or passed through here.

Finally, after what seemed like hours to Josh, he heard her splashing out of the creek.

Suddenly, the young woman screamed. "Indian! Indian! Indian!"

Chapter Twelve

Josh leaped to his feet and without taking time to yank on his boots, raced toward the thicket. Off to his left, he heard Tiny splashing upstream. When he slid to a halt in the clearing, Marylee had wrapped herself in her towel and was pointing to the unmoving body of a bare-chested Indian. She was still screaming.

"Quiet!" Josh demanded, cocking his .44 and easing toward the still form.

Marylee caught her breath, but stopped screaming.

The first thing Josh saw was the ragged exit wound on the Indian's back. Kiowa, Josh decided, noting the braided hair and the yellow and red war stripes on the one cheek he could see. He nudged the Kiowa with his toe, but the unconscious brave didn't move.

Wary as a bobcat, the lanky cowboy noted that the brave's outstretched hands held no weapons. He quickly knelt and slipped the Kiowa's war knife from its sheath.

By this time, Tiny had splashed ashore. "He dead?"

Josh didn't answer. Instead, using his toe, he turned the brave onto his back. The warrior's limp arms flopped lifelessly out to the side.

Marylee gasped and pressed her doubled fist to her lips when she saw the ugly black hole in the young man's chest, only inches above his heart. "Why, he's not much older than a child," she murmured.

"Old enough to take scalps," Tiny muttered darkly.

Keeping his .44 trained on the unconscious brave, Josh noted an almost imperceptible rising and falling of the Kiowa's chest. "He's alive." He holstered his Colt and nodded to Tiny. "Let's get him back to the wagon and see what we can do."

Stunned by Josh's eagerness to help a man who would gladly kill and scalp him, Marylee stared dumbfounded as Tiny effortlessly picked up the young warrior and carried him back to camp.

Josh hurried ahead putting water on to boil. He called over his shoulder to Marylee, "Get dressed and get some clean rags." He spread a blanket from his soogan on the ground in the shade of the wagon.

While Tiny gently laid the unconscious Kiowa on

the blanket, Josh fumbled in his saddlebags for his beaded parfleche bag. From it, he pulled out three smaller bags and dumped powder from each into a tin cup. He sprinkled water in the cup and stirred the ingredients into a paste.

While the concoction set, he chopped a petal of peyote into tiny pieces, then dropped them into another cup and filled it with an inch or so of water. "All right, Tiny. Lift his head."

The Kiowa's head lolled from side to side. Josh held him steady, wedged the lip of the cup between the warrior's lips, and slowly poured the contents down his throat. He coughed and sputtered once or twice, but kept most of the liquid down.

"What is that?" Marylee had come up behind them and was watching curiously.

"Peyote," Tiny whispered, gently lowering the young Indian's head. "Dulls the pain."

Josh washed the dirt from the wound on the young man's chest with hot water. "At least the slug went clean through," he muttered, concentrating on tending the wound. He stirred the stiff mixture in the cup once again, then pinched some with his fingers and worked it into the wound. He continued massaging and working two more pinches into the wound, and then turned the young warrior over, doing the same to the exit hole in his back.

"There," he muttered later as he tied the final knot in the bandage around the unconscious warrior's chest. "That ought to take care of him."

Since leaving Dodge City, Marylee's eastern sensibilities had taken a beating. A few days earlier, she would have felt little or no concern for a savage Indian, but now as she stared at the still features of the young man, she experienced a disquieting and puzzling sense of distress. "Will he be all right?"

"Yes, Miss," said Tiny. "Josh doctored him up good."

She stared at the unconscious warrior, reminding herself that he was nothing more than a savage. "What did you put on him? It didn't look like any medicine I've ever seen."

Josh stretched his arms above his head, and then reached for the coffee pot while Tiny explained. "Bark from the butternut and cottonwood trees all ground up along with some yellow monkey flower." He shook his head. "Reckon that'll either kill or cure about anything."

She frowned. "Where did you learn something like that?"

Winking at Tiny, Josh chuckled. "Back in East Texas, you learn a lot." He poured a cup of coffee. "We picked up the peyote medicine from a small band of Mimbreno Apaches we wintered with one year."

While she was pleased the Indian would survive, she still felt an aversion to the young man. He was a savage, and the sooner they shed themselves of him, the better she would like it, she reminded herself during the night.

To the dark-haired young woman's surprise when she emerged from her wagon next morning, the Kiowa brave was sitting up, leaning against the rear wheel of the lead wagon facing Josh.

Tiny sat by the fire, watching Josh and the Indian making sign.

She knelt by the fire, curious. "What are they doing?"

"Talking," Tiny replied, his voice low.

"Talking? I don't hear anything."

"Sign language. See their hands."

The brave was holding his right hand palm up, fingers curved slightly, and using only wrist action, scribing the hand back and forth. "That means Kiowa, a prairie Indian," the large cowpoke whispered. "Like we figured."

"What's Josh saying now?" she asked, referring to his linking the index finger of each hand in front of his chest.

"Friend. That's the southern tribes' way of saying friend."

The silent conversation continued for a few more

minutes until Josh rose and extended his arm, palm facing the Kiowa, and making a gentle downward motion.

"That means wait," Tiny volunteered.

Josh nodded to Marylee as he approached.

"So, how's the Indian?" she asked, her tone expressing her indifference.

"Good. Another day or so, he'll be up and around," he said, squatting and rolling up some beans in a johnnycake and pouring a cup of coffee. "While he's eating this, we'll get ready to move out." He glanced at Marylee. "You best eat a bite too, Miss."

The day was like those previous, a blistering sun baking the prairie, no breeze, and when a random gust did pass, it was oven hot.

Marylee pulled up alongside Josh at mid-morning and nodded to the Kiowa, who rode on top of the freight. "What are you going to do with the Indian?"

Josh sensed the disdain in her voice. He glanced at her and shrugged. "His name is Black Wolf. He's Kiowa, a young brave. I figure on giving him a horse as soon as he's fit and let him go back to his own people."

Her eyes opened in surprise. "You're what? But, he's a savage. Shouldn't you turn him over to the law?"

With a chuckle, Josh reminded her. "That boy's no

more savage than those white jaspers we've met up with since we've been gone from Dodge. Why, if I had to bet on which ones I could trust, I'd put my money on Black Wolf."

Disbelief edged her voice. "I don't believe it. You're really going to turn him loose so he can go out and murder white people?"

He studied her several moments, then decided against trying to make her understand. He nodded. "Yes," he replied simply.

Because of Black Wolf, they skirted Zulu Stockade and continued southwest across the Texas Panhandle, camping that night in the middle of a prairie flatter than a wet saddle blanket.

Black Wolf sat apart from the fire, leaning against the rear wheel of the lead wagon, aware of but unconcerned by the white woman's intense dislike for him.

Greedily, he ate the stew and johnnycakes and washed it all down with hot coffee sweetened with a handful of sugar.

Squatting on his haunches, Tiny stared at the fire. "We ought to hit Little Blue Stage Station tomorrow afternoon."

Josh glanced at Marylee. "After that, Miss, only another day until you're with your brothers."

She looked at his grimy clothes with distaste. "I

can't wait." She shook her head, her ringlets having straightened even more after her bath at Chiquita Creek. "I'll soak in a hot tub for a week with perfume water and bubbles."

"How long have you been gone from the ranch? I mean, back East," Josh asked.

Marylee shook her head. "I've never seen the ranch. My family lived in Missouri when I went back East to school. That was ten years ago. My mother died two years before when she gave birth to my youngest brother, Simon. My two older brothers, Matt and John, bought the ranch seven or eight years ago. They brought my two younger brothers, Luke and Simon, with them." She curled a lip. "They raise sheep and cows from what they say in their letters."

Josh frowned. "But, the Winchester the other day. And you don't ride like a tenderfoot."

For the first time since they met, she smiled warmly. "My pa—I mean, my father taught me to ride and hunt back in Missouri."

Tiny chuckled. "That explains it, then." He poured another cup of coffee. "This is a mighty hard country out here for a lady like you. It'll take a heap of getting used to."

"Oh," she replied airily. "I don't plan on staying. It's just for a visit so I can get my dowry from my brothers." She eyed the countryside around them distastefully. "I'd rather die than spend the rest of my life in such a forsaken and barren country. It's so cruel. Killing one another. I could never do that. I'm just coming for a visit, and then I'm traveling on to San Francisco where my fiancé, Oliver Van Dort, is waiting."

The announcement surprised Josh. For some reason, he had never imagined she would have a fiancé anywhere. On the other hand, he told himself, she was a fine-looking lady even if she had the temperament of a she-wolf protecting her cubs.

"Well, Miss Marylee," Tiny replied, dumping the rest of his coffee on the fire. "I hope everything goes your way."

Josh rose to his feet. "Reckon it's time to roll into our soogans. I want to get a early start."

Later as the fire burned down, Tiny whispered in the darkness. "Josh, what's one of them dowry things?"

The lanky cowpoke grinned to himself. "That's where the family gives the daughter to be married a heap of money."

Tiny didn't reply. Just as Josh started to doze off, Tiny spoke up again. "Why do they do that? I mean give her money. They ain't so hard up to marry her off that they got to pay some jasper to take her, are they?"

Josh, half asleep, muttered, "No. It isn't like that. I'll explain it tomorrow. Now go to sleep."

"All right, but it sure don't make much sense to me."

Knowing they were within two days of Atascocita, the small party pulled out next morning with buoyed spirits. Even the mules sensed the end of the journey was near—Ulysses, the near leader, kept trying to pick up the pace.

His wound healing quickly, Black Wolf sat on the lead wagon, his keen eyes watching for the slightest alien movement out on the prairie.

Ten miles ahead at a shinnery patch at the base of the caprock, Big Nose Crawford rose from a small campfire and slurped a slug of coffee from a tin mug and studied the gunhands he had hired. He nodded to a slender German, whose blue eyes were cold as ice. "Litz, ride up the trail. See if you can spot the wagons." He nodded to the others. "Barker, you and Swede there know where your hiding spot is just below the caprock on either side of the trail. Me and Harrigan will stay here in the shinnery. Remember, we don't want to leave no one alive."

"What about the bodies?" Swede said.

"Leave them for the buzzards. They won't last a day." Crawford looked around. "Any other questions?"

A few grunts came from the grizzled band. Harrigan muttered, "I'll be mighty glad when this is over. I'm going to drink me a whole barrel of whiskey."

"Not me," growled Barker. "I'm going to find me someplace that has good company."

Crawford laughed. "I'll buy it for you if you do me a good job here."

Chapter Thirteen

After a noon break, the wagons pushed southwest along the well-worn Jones-Plummer Trail. The scorching sun beat down, tempered only by the gentle southern breeze that despite its heat, at least stirred the air.

Tiny pulled up next to Josh. "Best I recollect, the caprock's only a couple miles ahead. After that is Little Blue Stage Station." He patted his iron-hard belly. "I reckon I could put myself around a couple of them steaks old Mort fries up."

He glanced at Black Wolf, who was sitting cross-legged on the wagon. "How's he doing?"

Josh raised an eyebrow. "He's probably in better shape than you and me." He laughed and nodded to Black Wolf, who returned his nod.

"You mean what you told her about letting him go?"

Josh frowned.

With a grin, Tiny explained. "She came to me to help. She couldn't believe you wasn't going to turn him over to the law. When I told her I agreed with you, then she got mad at me."

Shaking his head, Josh groaned. "Don't try to figure her out. She's from the East. That's a whole different world back there." He laughed. "There's only two ways to handle them easterners, and neither one of them works."

Squatting around the small campfire behind the patch of oak shinnery, Crawford and the other hardcases waited, drinking coffee and smoking cigarettes. "Sure wish they'd hurry up and get here," growled Barker. "I'm getting saddle sores just a'sitting."

Before any of the owlhoots could reply, a whooping yell sounded from the top of the caprock. Crawford jumped to his feet as Litz came boiling down the steep trail, kicking up clouds of dust. "They're coming, they're coming," he shouted, slapping his hat against the rump of his pony. He jerked his horse to a sliding halt.

"How far?" Crawford asked.

Litz jabbed his arm in the direction of the wagons. "Maybe a couple miles."

"That's it, boys. Find your spots. Litz, you find a

hidey-hole at the top of the caprock behind one of them boulders. When they get halfway down, boys, blow them apart."

What Litz didn't tell them was that with the high-powered telescope he carried in his saddlebags, he had seen a woman on the last wagon, and it had been months since he had been with a woman.

Black Wolf sat upright on the top of the wagon, peering to the south at the faint cloud of dust. Too thick to be raised by an animal other than a horse or cow.

He glanced at the white man on the mule, wondering if he also noticed the thin veil of dust. A prickling of worry nagged at him, raising the hair on the back of his neck. He eased to the front of the wagon and grunted loud enough to catch Josh's attention.

The sun-browned cowpoke looked around and frowned. He pointed to the Kiowa's chest. "Hurt?"

Black Wolf shook his head and extended his arm with the back of his hand up and fingers pointing to the left. He made a quick movement to the right, at the same time turning his thumb up.

Josh understood. He repeated the gesture, saying, "Enemy?"

Not understanding the white man's language, Black Wolf repeated the gesture, then motioned for Josh to rein up.

When he did, Tiny came riding back. "What's going on?"

"Black Wolf here says something is wrong up ahead."

Tiny frowned. "Like what?"

Before Josh could reply, the Kiowa brave descended from the wagon, motioned for them to remain still and, holding his hand over his chest, went ahead on foot, studying the ground.

A few moments later, Marylee approached. "What are we stopping for? I don't want to waste any more time than necessary."

Josh explained Black Wolf's concern.

The young woman sneered. "I don't see how you could trust him. He's probably leading us into a trap set by his own people."

Tiny glared at her. "Well, we'll soon know. Here he comes."

A red stain was spreading on the bandage on Black Wolf's chest, but he refused any aid until he told them he had found tracks, fresh tracks that had suddenly turned back within the last thirty minutes.

"So what does that mean?" Marylee asked, obviously unimpressed with the information returned by the Kiowa.

Black Wolf touched a finger to his nostrils, then

pointed to Josh and Tiny and gestured south along the trail.

Tiny grimaced. "Blast it, Josh. I think he's saying there's white men up ahead."

"Of course there are," the impatient young woman put in. "What's the name of the place, Little Blue Stage Station?"

Josh removed his hat and ran his fingers through his dark hair. "Could be that's all it is, but then why would some jasper turn back so sudden-like." He paused, then added, "Unless, he saw something and didn't want it to see him."

Tiny arched an eyebrow. "Kinda stretching things aren't you, partner?"

Grinning sheepishly, Josh shrugged. "I'd rather stretch something that isn't there than get stretched out on the ground by something that is there."

Tiny shucked his big Spencer rifle. Josh tossed Black Wolf his Winchester and turned to Marylee. "You best get back in your wagon, Miss. Stay low, hold tight, and don't stick your head out."

"Follow me," said Tiny, reining his blood bay a few feet in front of the team.

"If there is trouble, partner," Josh called out, "we're going through. Don't rein up, or I'll run over you."

As they rattled along the trail, Josh's brain raced. The only way off the Staked Plains was the trail ahead—the only trail down for miles in either direction. Thick cedar and large boulders flanked either side of the narrow road. If trouble jumped them, that's where it would be hiding.

Tiny remained just in front of the team as they slowly approached the edge of the caprock. When they were less than a hundred yards from the rim, Black Wolf grunted.

Josh reined up. "What is it?"

The Kiowa warrior's nostrils flared. He pointed to where the trail disappeared over the caprock.

Puzzled, Josh whispered, "Men are there? Waiting there?"

Black Wolf frowned.

Tiny rode up as Josh hurriedly extended his arm to the Kiowa, pointing his index finger forward and up, the sign for male. Then he nodded in the direction Black Wolf had indicated.

Black Wolf nodded in return.

Josh looked at Tiny. "We've got us a reception committee ahead."

Tiny's face grew hard. He cocked the hammer on his Spencer and grinned at Josh. "Then let's us don't keep them waiting."

Glancing around, Josh spotted Marylee watching from the pucker hole in the canvas, a puzzled frown on her face. He waved her back, then dismounted and fashioned a set of reins on Ulysses' bridle before swinging up on the mule's back.

He had never used a jerk-line on galloping mules. He'd have more control with reins if there was trouble or if they were forced into a gallop.

Tiny sidled up to Josh. With a reckless grin on his square face, he said, "Ready, partner?"

Josh grinned and tugged his Stetson down on his head. "Ready."

Tiny led out, staying several yards ahead of the team.

Josh shucked his Colt and cocked the hammer. Ahead of him, Tiny sat easy in his saddle, warily studying the surrounding countryside.

Beyond, the prairie dropped over a hundred feet to rolling sandhills covered with sage. The sharp scent of cedar drifted up the slope, stinging his nostrils. It was a spectacular sight, the stark beauty of which always fascinated Josh, but this time, it sent chills racing up his spine.

Tiny started down, and moments later, the team followed, clattering on the rocks. Josh leaned back to keep his balance as the mules picked their way down the steep, rocky slope.

Boulders and cedar crowded in on either side.

Josh kept his eyes moving, peering into the cedar for

even the slightest movement, all the while in the back of his mind hoping they were spooked over nothing.

Without warning, a chilling war cry ripped from Black Wolf's throat, and he began firing the Winchester. Josh jerked around at a scream from his left, and a bearded *hombre* spun out of the cedar to sprawl on the ground.

Gunfire erupted from every side.

Ulysses needed no urging from Josh. The mule broke into a gallop down the trail. Slugs whipped past as the wagons clattered and shuddered, iron rims clanging like church bells over the rocky slope, picking up speed.

Ahead, Tiny sat upright in his saddle, clenching the reins in his teeth and firing the Spencer as quickly as he could chamber another cartridge.

As the trailing wagon shot past, Litz leaped from behind a cedar and lunged for the tailgate, imagining what pleasures were in store for him behind the closed canvas. He pulled himself up on the tailgate, and with a leer on his lips, stuck his head through the pucker hole.

When he saw Marylee, he leered. "Well, look here. A nice, sweet little—" Next thing he knew, a searing pain ripped into his cheek. He screamed and threw himself backward, bouncing along the rocky trail until his head slammed into a boulder, crushing his skull.

Chapter Fourteen

The cedar on either side blurred as the wagon shot past, the wooden wheels narrowly missing the rugged boulders along the trail. Leaning low over the neck of his near leader, Josh clutched the reins in one hand while firing at the puffs of smoke erupting from behind the boulders and among the cedar. From somewhere behind, cutting through the booming reports of the Winchester in Black Wolf's hands, he thought he heard Marylee scream.

Suddenly, they swept past the shinnery patch and out onto the prairie where Josh reined the mules around sharply, stopping the wagons in the shape of an L. He leaped from the mule as Tiny came sliding up and dismounted in a swirling cloud of dust, quickly removing and then inserting another loaded cartridge tube in the butt of the Spencer.

Marylee peered through the pucker hole, her face blanched with fear. "Get down here," Josh yelled. He looked around for Black Wolf, but the Kiowa was nowhere to be seen. "Blast," he muttered.

"Where'd he go? Black Wolf, I mean," Tiny asked.

Hastily reloading his Colt, Josh shrugged. "No idea. He was firing, and then he was gone."

"You reckon he's dead?"

Josh didn't know, but he did figure it was mighty peculiar that Black Wolf had sensed trouble ahead like he had. Before the lanky cowpoke could answer or express his suspicions concerning the Kiowa warrior, Marylee stumbled up, breathless. "Who—"

"Are you all right?" Josh demanded, interrupting her. "You screamed!"

She nodded. "Yes, but—"

Ignoring her, he clambered over the side of the wagon and fished another Winchester from under the seat and jammed it in her hands. "Here, take this. You know how to use it. You take the end of the wagon. Tiny'll stay here. I'll go down to the other end."

Her eyes grew wide. "You mean, you want me to—"

The wiry cowboy glared at her, his patience stretched tighter than a boil. "I want you to stay alive, and if that means shooting somebody, then lady, you best shoot somebody." He glared at her a few more seconds, then turned on his heel.

From behind the wagon, Josh studied the trail down the caprock. He saw no movement. The air was still and hot, tinged with the leathery smell of mule sweat. Abruptly, a bloodcurdling scream from the rocky slope split the silence and echoed across the rolling prairie.

Behind him, he heard Marylee gasp.

All grew silent once again. The sun baked the lanky cowpoke's shoulders, burned his neck. He blinked against the sweat running down his forehead, stinging his eyes. Minutes later, the blazing silence was shattered by a single shot, and within moments Black Wolf appeared from the patch of shinnery. He held up a hand holding a bloody knife, but didn't move.

Keeping his Colt cocked, Josh waved the slender brave to the wagons, still suspicious. As Black Wolf drew near, Josh looked at the knife in the brave's hand.

With a sneer, the Kiowa wiped the blade on his naked thigh and sheathed it. He gestured to the trail, then extended his left hand, back out, fingers extended and bent to the right. He made a forward and out motion.

"What's he saying?" asked Tiny as he and Marylee approached.

Josh felt his cheeks burn for his earlier suspicions. "He says those bushwhackers there are all dead." He spoke to Black Wolf. "How many?" he asked, holding up his fingers. "One, two, three . . ."

With a puzzled frown, Black Wolf shook his head and gestured back to the trail.

"Tiny, you stay here with Miss Marylee. Black Wolf and me are going back and see just who those jaspers were."

When they returned fifteen minutes later, they were leading four horses, gunbelts looped over the horns and rifles in the boots. Josh tied the ponies to the tailgate of the trailing wagon and tossed the guns in the back of the wagon. "Five of them. Looks like we got three on the way down." He paused and gave Marylee a crooked grin. "Well, maybe two. One of the *hombres* was in the middle of the road. His skull smashed, but what was so peculiar was that he had a lady's hat pin jammed in his cheek."

Tiny exclaimed. "What?"

Nodding slowly, Josh folded his arms over his chest and looked at Marylee, whose cheeks were turning crimson. She dropped her gaze to the sandy ground at her feet. "That's right," Josh replied with an amused smile on his face. "A hat pin. Now how do you figure that jasper could run into a woman's hat pin all the way out here in the Texas Panhandle?"

She straightened her shoulders and glared at Josh.

"All right. I did it, but that—that creature was trying to climb into the wagon. He was dirty and his teeth were black. And what he said—" She closed her eyes, hugged herself, and shivered. Then she looked back up into Josh's face defiantly. "There was no way I would let him touch me."

A sense of self-reproach washed over Josh for teasing her. He smiled gently. "I understand, Miss Marylee. You just did what you had to do. Polecats like that don't give decent people a choice. It is a hard world out here, and maybe you're right to go on to San Francisco and get away from this."

"He's right, Miss," said Tiny. "Don't blame yourself. That one might have hurt you something bad." He paused and gestured to the horses. "You said there were five, Josh. What happened to the other horse?"

Josh shrugged. "Spooked away by the shooting, I suppose." He looked at the sun. "We've wasted enough daylight with those jaspers and all this palavering. It's time we get moving if we want to reach Little Blue Stage Station tonight."

Black Wolf laid his hand on Josh's arm, staying him from climbing up on the near wheeler. He pointed to his own chest, then back north, and made the up and down motion with his hand that signaled he was leaving.

Josh nodded, and offered his hand, grasping Black

Wolf's. He linked his index fingers in front of his chest once again, then pointed to the four horses and indicated the Kiowa warrior take two of them as well as a Winchester and ammunition.

"He sure didn't argue none, did he?" Tiny observed as they watched Black Wolf ride up the caprock leading a sorrel.

"Never known an Indian who wouldn't take what was offered him or what he thought he deserved."

When Black Wolf reached the rim of the caprock, he pulled up and held his hand high.

Josh returned the farewell.

Marylee looked on, strangely silent, and strangely puzzled. She understood just what had taken place, the gesture of friendship and thanks. That, she could accept, but not between a white man and an Indian.

Ten minutes later, Black Wolf reined up. In the distance, he spotted a riderless horse with a fancy saddle inlaid with silver grazing on sparse grass. A faint smile broke the stoic expression on his face. To return with three horses and such a saddle would do much to elevate him in the eyes of the Koitsenko, the warrior society comprised of the ten bravest warriors in the tribe.

The weary party reached Little Blue Stage Station just before dusk. A mothering Mrs. Helitzer ushered

Marylee inside for a hot bath. Outside, Josh and Tiny tended the animals as they told Mort Helitzer about the bushwhacking.

The older man sucked on a tooth. "I ain't seen no group like that riding past, not in the last two weeks. You think they was really waiting for you old boys or just lying in wait for any unsuspecting soul?"

Josh shook his head. "Got no idea."

The last few miles into Atascocita seemed to take months instead of mere hours.

Finally, they spotted the small village, a collection of clapboard, canvas, and adobe buildings. The town was smaller than Josh remembered it, but when he saw Buckalew's livery, he felt like he was home.

Frenchy rushed out to meet them when they pulled into the corral, exuberant that they had made it safely with the goods. Even before Josh climbed off his mule, she was saying, "We was worried. There's been a heap of talk about Kiowa and Comancheros raiding all through the Panhandle and Indian Territory. Why—"

Her words stuck in her throat when she saw Marylee emerge from the trailing wagon. She looked up at Josh, who explained. "Frenchy, meet Miss Marylee Gaston. She decided she wanted to ride with us instead of the stage," he said with a grin.

Frenchy scurried back to help Marylee down from

the wagon. "Lordy, Lordy, child. We was all worried about you. Figured you had changed your mind when you didn't come in on the stage. We didn't know what to do," she said, her words coming out so fast they tumbled over each other. "Come on inside, child. Get out of this heat. I have some cool well water in the office. Give you a chance to freshen up." As she ushered Marylee inside, she shot a worried glance over her shoulder at Josh and then closed the office door behind her.

Josh frowned, puzzled over the cryptic expression on her face. Moments later, his frown deepened when George Buckalew hurried out of the office, a troubled look on his wrinkled face. He headed for the street as fast as his frail legs and walking cane permitted. Josh stopped him. "What's going on, George? What's the rush?"

He shook his head and tugged his hat down on his head. "Can't talk now. I got to get Preacher Millsap."

"The preacher?" Josh glanced at Tiny, who shrugged. "What do you need the preacher for?"

George hesitated and turned to Josh. He nodded to the office. "Somebody's got to tell that little girl in there that her brothers are dead, murdered by thieving Comancheros."

Chapter Fifteen

"All we know," Buckalew explained after Reverend Millsap went inside, "about two weeks after you boys pulled out, we got word her two older brothers was found dead. The two younger ones is staying out at the Newton Ranch."

Josh loosened the ropes holding the canvas cover over the freight. "Sure hate to hear that." He glanced at the office, a sorrowful knit to his brow. "She's a mighty opinionated lady, but something like that shouldn't happen to anyone. They find the killers?"

The old man shook his head. "Got clean away. Probably after the gold coins the brothers was said to have hid." He hesitated, then changed the subject. "How was the trip? Any trouble?"

Tiny chuckled. "A tad, I reckon."

The old man's frown deepened as Josh and Tiny related the events surrounding the ambush.

The wizened old gentleman cut off a twist of tobacco and poked it in his cheek. He leaned on his cane. "Five you say? Recognize any?"

Tiny gathered the gunbelts and rifles that had belonged to the dead bushwhackers from the rear of the lead wagon while Josh untied the two horses from the trailing wagon. "Never seen them before. They didn't look like Comancheros. We figure that they was probably just owlhoots waiting for a plump chicken to come along."

George glanced at the gunbelts in Tiny's arms, then nodded to C. L. Freight across the street. "I got no proof, but it sure as the dickens has got the smell of Cullen Leach all over it worser than stink on a skunk."

"You figure he'd go that far, huh, George?" Tiny asked.

The old man nodded emphatically. "Bet your last cent. I still think Leach was behind the barn burning. But, like the bushwhacking, I got no proof. And even if I did, I don't know that it would do much good."

Josh frowned. "You talking about the sheriff? He seemed like a right honest sort."

Buckalew snorted. "Oh, Dan Ellis is honest as the day is long. It's the district judge. There's no one, alive that is, that can prove it, but the feeling is Cullen Leach carries Judge Toler in his back pocket. Rumor is that Toler is a silent partner in Leach's freight business."

Shaking his head, Josh replied, "There must be something you could do."

"If there is, it beats me." He paused a moment. "Them bushwhackers out there. Can you describe them?"

The younger cowpoke looked up at his partner. "Not really. They was just average saddle tramps. Nothing unusual that I could see."

Suddenly, the older man blinked, then stared at the gunbelts Tiny held. He reached out and slipped a pearl-handled Colt from one holster. "This belong to one of them?" He looked up expectantly.

Josh sensed a touch of excitement in the elderly man's voice. "Yep. Why?"

The old man peered up at Josh. "You must've seen them dead bushwhackers, huh?"

"Yes."

"One of them have a big nose?" He touched the muzzle of the revolver to his nose.

Josh shrugged. "Hard to say. One of them had part of his face blowed away. And I don't recollect any thing real noticeable about their noses. Why?"

George turned the revolver over in his hands and

then looked over at C. L. Freight. "Because, this six-gun looks like the one Big Nose Crawford carries. He's always polishing them pearl handles."

Tiny frowned. "Crawford? Who's he?"

With grim satisfaction, George replied, "Cullen Leach's right-hand gunnie. Remember the sorrel with the silver inlaid saddle that come in with the mules that time?"

Josh nodded.

"Well, that pony and saddle belonged to Big Nose Crawford."

At that moment, Reverend Millsap emerged from the office and, wearing a solemn expression on his face, came over to where the three men stood.

Josh asked, "How is she?"

"As well as could be expected. It was quite a shock. She's resting now. When Doc Nicholson gets back to town this afternoon, I'll have him send something to help her sleep."

George Buckalew spoke up. "We got laudanum, Preacher. A spoonful of that should calm her down some."

Across the street at C. L. Freight, Cullen Leach glared out the dingy window at the two wagons sitting in the corral, his plump face turning red with anger. What the blazes went wrong? Big Nose Craw-ford had pulled off dozens of ambushes. He shook his head in frustration and yanked the half-smoked cigar from his thick lips and rapped his knuckles on the window to catch the attention of Dave Rynning and Mad Tom Gristy, who were lounging on the porch, also eyeing the wagons.

He motioned them inside.

"Yes, sir, Mr. Leach," said Gristy, a wary look on his face.

Leach jabbed a sausage-thick finger at the wag-ons. "Something went wrong."

Rynning grunted and laid a hand on the butt of his six-gun. "We figured that when the wagons come in. What do you reckon happened to Big Nose?"

"That's what I want to know. You boys ride out to the caprock on the other side of Little Blue Stage Station. See if you can find out what took place out there." He stroked his chin. "I got a feeling they ran into a buzz saw with them two jaspers across the street yonder."

Rynning nodded, his face impassive. "Whatever you say, Mr. Leach."

"And don't leave nothing lying around that can connect to me, you understand?"

Mad Tom Cristy nodded. "Yes, sir."

The portly businessman smoothed his vest and

tugged on the lapels of his coat. "In the meantime, I'll see what I can find out."

Hats in hand, Josh and Tiny tiptoed into the office behind George. Frenchy met them at the kitchen door and touched her finger to her lips. "She's resting in the bedroom. I gave her a dose of laudanum. She'll sleep for a while, the poor child." Tucking loose strands of her gray hair into the bun on the back of her head, she gestured to the table. "Sit. I'll get the coffee. Now, you tell me what took place."

Josh swung his leg over the back of the straight-back chair and straddled the seat. Resting his arms on the back of the chair, he quickly outlined the events of the last few weeks finishing up with the bushwhacking.

"I'll say one thing for Miss Marylee," he whispered as Frenchy poured their coffee with her quirt dangling from her wrist. "She might be stubborn as a knot-headed mule, but she blasted well stood up good when those jaspers jumped us."

"Yes, ma'am," Tiny put in. "Why, she even jabbed one old boy in the face with a hat pin."

"A hat pin, you say." Frenchy laughed. "Maybe then she's still got something down inside that eastern learning couldn't take out of her." She shook her head. "I hope so, because she's going to need it now that she's been hit between the eyes with the news of her brothers."

George interrupted. "It was Leach's gunnies—"

"What's that?" Frenchy jerked around and glared at him.

The wizened old man nodded emphatically and continued, "—that bushwhacked these boys." He laid the pearl-handled revolver on the table. "The boys here took this off one of them hardcases."

Frenchy's eyes grew wide. "Why, that looks like the one Big Nose Crawford carried," she muttered in disbelief. And then she cut loose with a stream of obscenities that would have put many a muleskinner to shame. Her eyes blazed. "I've got a good mind to go over there and—"

"Whoa. Hold on there," Josh said. "Best thing is to turn it over to the sheriff. Let's make sure this Crawford jasper is the one who owned it." He glanced at Tiny and added, "Tiny and me have seen pearl-handled six-guns like that in a heap of places."

The older woman studied him a moment, then shrugged in resignation. "Reckon that's what we need to do."

"Now," Josh asked, "just what did happen to her brothers?"

George shifted the chaw of tobacco from one leathery cheek to the other and glanced under the table for his spittoon.

"It's on the other side, you old fool," Frenchy said, smiling patiently and shaking her head as she poured the coffee.

George picked up a gallon can, squirted a brown stream of tobacco juice in it, dragged the back of his hand over his lips and said, "According to Colas Vincente, the old Mex who told the sheriff about it, he was tending Gaston sheep when he spotted a dozen or so riders heading toward the ranch house. He hid. When they passed, he saw they were Comancheros. He recognized the leader, Sosthenes Archiveque, a no-good, murdering son of the Devil if there ever was one." He paused to spit again.

Impatiently Frenchy took over. "When Colas got to the main house, he found Matt and Josh Gaston dead, each shot in the back of the head. The place was torn apart. Searching for the gold, probably."

Tiny leaned forward. "Gold?"

"Coin," George said, taking over. "It's a fact that when the Gastons come in and bought the spread and stocked it with sheep and cattle, they paid for it with gold Double Eagles. Rumor is the gold is what they brought in from the California gold fields. The rest of the gold coins, about a thousand Double Eagles, they was supposed to have buried."

Josh whistled softly. "That's twenty thousand dollars."

Frenchy snorted. "Which I don't believe. Not that much. I figure it was all just a heap of wishful thinking on some folks' part. Oh, I grant you them Gastons had a stash of gold coin, but not that much," she retorted, giving her husband an I-told-you-so look.

Josh whistled softly. "So that's where she was going to get the money."

Frenchy raised her eyebrows in surprise. "What's that?"

Tiny nodded. "Miss Marylee, she said she was just coming for a visit. On the way to meet her fiancé out in San Francisco, but first she had to stop for her d-d—" The large man looked to Josh for help. "What was that she called it, Josh?"

"Dowry."

George Buckalew grinned at his wife. "A dowry, huh? See! That proves them Gaston boys was pretty well fixed."

Frenchy snapped. "Hush up, old man."

With a smug smile on his face, George Buckalew crossed his frail arms over his chest and leaned back in his chair.

"But," Josh said, "she still has two brothers. Isn't that right?"

"That'll be Luke and Simon. They're twelve and thirteen. They're staying at the Newton Ranch. They was visiting a neighboring ranch when the Comancheros hit," Frenchy replied. "Otherwise . . ." Her voice trailed off.

A knock at the door interrupted them. Frenchy opened the door and snorted. "Cullen Leach! Now what the Sam Hill are you doing here?"

Leach entered jovially, greeting George brightly. "Why, Frenchy, I just wanted to congratulate you on your wagons making it in all in one piece. With them Kiowas on the warpath, it took some doing to get your load through." He shook his head. "I must admit, I didn't think you could do it, but you fooled me. I was worried you might run into trouble."

The middle-aged woman eyed him shrewdly, recognizing his fawning words for what they were, an effort to learn just what had happened out on the trail. She narrowed her eyes and jammed her fists into her ample hips. Her words were sharp and hard. "Don't hand me that line of cow patties, Cullen Leach. There's nothing better you'd like than to see us run into trouble. You're so blasted greedy that you want all of the freight business around here even though there's more than enough to go around. And don't you deny it."

Tugging at the lapels of his brown striped suit, he laughed nervously. "Now, Frenchy. You know that isn't true. I want us all to work and thrive here in Atascocita together. We're all friends."

Frenchy exploded. "Friends my hind quarter. If that's true, why did you send Big Nose Crawford out to the caprock to bushwhack these boys here?" She gestured with her quirt at Josh and Tiny.

Leach's flabby face blanched. He shook his head emphatically, his jowls flopping, his brain racing. "Why, you're mistaken, Frenchy. I didn't send anyone out for anything."

She eyed him narrowly. "You're trying to tell me that you didn't send a bunch of owlhoots out to Little Blue Stage Station to bushwhack these boys and steal my wagons?" She knew he would never admit the truth, but she couldn't resist letting him know he wasn't fooling her or anyone else in Atascocita.

"Of course not," he sputtered, his flabby cheeks turning red. "Why would I do that?"

She jabbed her quirt at him. "I'll tell you why, Cullen Leach. For the same reason you had my barn burned last month. You want me and George out of business."

"Th-that's preposterous," he stammered, eyeing the shaking tip of the quirt warily.

"Is it?" Her eyes blazed. "Where's that gunnie of

yours, Crawford? I ain't seen him around in the last few days."

A sheen of sweat glistened on his forehead. "Why, I sent him to Hidetown to buy a load of buffalo robes. There's a growing market for them up in Wichita." He glanced nervously at Josh and Tiny.

She snorted. "Don't take us for fools, Cullen Leach. He bushwhacked my boys. Got hisself killed dead." She pointed to the revolver on the table. "They took this off one of the bushwhackers. It's Crawford's hogleg."

The corpulent man glanced at the revolver. He tried to appear indifferent, but his shifting eyes betrayed him. "I don't know about no ambush, but if Crawford was part of one, he deserves whatever he got." He hesitated, then added, "I'd have to see for myself before I'd believe that he was part of it. He's rough, I grant you, but he's always been honest to me." He nodded to the revolver. "Besides, there's pearl-handled guns all over the state. Anyone could have one. That's no proof."

Jerking her quirt over her head, she took a threatening step toward him. "He wasn't, huh? Well, I tell you what, Cullen Leach. We're going to go out there and bring them bodies back. And then we'll see who's telling the truth, and who's lying."

Regaining his composure, Leach smiled thinly.

"Well now, Frenchy, that's a dandy idea. You go right ahead. Maybe we can get to the bottom of this, but one thing for sure, you can't hook me up with that bushwhacking because I had nothing to do with it. And I don't think Crawford did either." He turned to Tiny and Josh. "That's the truth, boys. Bring the bodies in. See for yourself."

Josh studied the smiling businessman. He seemed mighty confident. Was it possible the six-gun did not belong to Big Nose Crawford, and Cullen Leach was telling the truth?

Chapter Sixteen

As soon as the door shut behind Cullen Leach, Frenchy pointed her quirt at Josh. "You boys hook up the buckboard. Light a shuck out there and bring them bodies back."

Josh hooked his thumb over his shoulder. "What about the wagons, Frenchy? Don't you want us to unload them first?"

Smoothing her graying hair unconsciously, she looked out the window at the two freight wagons. "No. They'll stay dry in the livery. Besides, there's no hurry now. Most of the goods were the Gastons. With the brothers dead, I don't know what we'll do with what they ordered. . . ." Her voice trailed off, and she shook her head wearily.

Josh and Tiny exchanged concerned looks.

154

* * *

Thirty minutes later, with Josh on the buckboard and Tiny astride his blood bay, they headed north out of Atascocita.

Across the street, Leach peered through the front window of his freight office and sneered as he watched the two cowpokes disappear into the clouds of dust swirling up about them at the end of the street. "Have fun, boys," Leach grunted in a mocking voice. He pulled out a black cigar and clipped off the tip.

Tiny sat easily in the saddle. He looked down at his partner. "What do you reckon Frenchy was getting at back there?"

"Nothing good. She was counting on this shipment to keep her in business. If she can't find a buyer for the goods, well, I reckon they might have to close up the freight end of their business."

"Blazes," Tiny growled. "I hope not. They're good people." After a few minutes, Tiny said, "I just figured out what we ought to do for Frenchy and George. Maybe get them over this hump they're facing."

Keeping his eyes on the road ahead, Josh grunted. "Oh? And just what might that be?"

"It was mighty decent of them to help us out of our bind. I reckon we could pay back their kindness by giving them the two hundred and fifty dollars we won up in Dodge City."

Josh looked up sharply. "We won? What do you mean, *we* won? I won it."

Tiny shrugged. "Maybe so, but I let you keep playing. I could have stopped you by busting up the place."

"Yeah, you could have, and got us tossed in the hoosegow."

"But I didn't. So what do you think?"

Josh felt the roll of bills in his pocket pressing against his leg. He drew a deep breath and slowly released it. Two hundred and fifty dollars was eight or nine month's wages. Suppressing a grin, he glanced sidelong at Tiny. "I got to think on it."

Tiny failed to see the teasing gleam in Josh's eyes. He snorted. "Well, don't think too long."

The waxing moon had risen by the time Tiny and Josh rode into Little Blue Stage Station. During the early morning hours, a steady rain settled over the rolling countryside. The rain was still falling when they rose next morning.

"Looks like this could be an all-day affair," Tiny muttered, staring up at the leaden skies while he tightened the cinch about the belly of his blood bay.

Josh joked. "Don't worry. You won't melt."

"Well, what did you decide?"

Feigning ignorance, Josh replied, "Decide? About what?"

Tiny eyed him skeptically. "You know what. The poker winnings."

Josh shook his head and chuckled. "What do you think I decided? Same as you. I figured it was a good idea when you mentioned it."

Resting his arms on the saddle and leaning forward over the blood bay, Tiny glared at Josh. "Why didn't you say something then?"

Josh climbed onto the buckboard seat and popped the reins on the rumps of the team. "Because I didn't want you to get a big head for coming up with such a good idea."

Tiny grinned and swung into the saddle.

The rain had subsided to a drizzle by the time they rolled back into Atascocita that afternoon. Frenchy hurried outside to meet the buckboard. She stared at the empty bed in disbelief, the rain dripping off the wide brim of her floppy hat.

Tiny dismounted. "The bodies were gone, Frenchy. Flat gone."

"He's right. At first we thought that coyotes or wolves might have worried them off, but we searched for a quarter-mile around. The rain washed out all sign. Someone moved them," Josh said, unhitching the two bays from the buckboard.

Frenchy muttered a soft curse. "Leach!"

Josh cut his eyes toward the office. "How's Miss Marylee today?"

She grimaced, her eyes fixed on the empty buckboard bed. "I sure was hoping to find Crawford." She slapped her quirt against her thigh and drew a deep breath. "Oh, well, I reckon worse things have happened." She looked up at Josh. "Huh? What did you say?"

"Miss Marylee. She up and around today?"

"Yes. Poor thing. Still shocked, but she seems to be handling it well. Sent word out to the Newton place that she was here. She wants to go out there tomorrow. Reckon you boys can take her?"

While Josh sympathized with Marylee's loss, he wasn't any too anxious to spend any more time around her and her stuck-up ways. "I suppose, but shouldn't one of us hang around here? Not all of the shipment was Gaston's. Don't we need to unload the other folks'?"

"No need. Them that had goods come in today and unloaded it theirselves. No, I'd feel better if both you boys went with her."

*   *   *

Across the muddy street, Leach smirked. "Well, boys. You done a good job," he said to Rynning and Gristy who stood at his side. "Too bad about Crawford though," he added indifferently.

Gristy grinned, but the expression on Rynning's was impassive. "A good thing the rain came. It must have washed out all sign showing where we dragged the bodies to a gully a half-mile from the trail."

Gristy shuddered. "The animals and buzzards had already done a good job on them waddies. Another day, and there won't be nothing left but bones."

Grinning expansively, Leach shrugged. "Now they got no proof."

That evening around the kitchen table, Marylee announced that as soon as she could sell the ranch and take care of matters at the bank, she and her two younger brothers were heading for California.

Josh glanced at Frenchy, who was chewing on her lip. He knew the announcement meant the end of Buckalew Freight to the older woman. He grimaced. His own mother had died in childbirth, but he had a feeling that she might have been a lot like Frenchy.

With a puzzled frown on his face, Tiny said, "What about them that killed your brothers, Miss Marylee. The Comanchero they call So—so—"

"Sosthenes Archiveque," George volunteered.

"Yeah. That one. Don't you want to see him hanged before you leave?"

She looked at Tiny, her lips curled in disgust. "I don't want to see anyone killed, and I don't want to stay in this country any longer than I have to. Tomorrow, we'll ride out to the ranch and bring the boys back in," she added haughtily.

The rain passed during the night, and the sun rose next morning in a freshly washed blue sky. When Marylee came out of the livery office, Josh blinked in surprise. She was wearing a high-necked, cinched-waist blue dress that swept the ground. Frenchy tagged after her, and when the older woman saw the skepticism in Josh's eyes, she simply shrugged helplessly.

Josh helped the young woman into the front seat of the two-seat fringed surrey. "You look right fetching this morning, Miss Marylee, but I'm afraid you might get mighty uncomfortable later on in the day in that outfit. It looks to be a hot day."

She smiled coolly at him. "I'll be just fine, thank you."

With a resigned shake of his head, Josh gee-hawed the team. Apparently, he told himself, she hadn't learned a blasted thing on the trip down from Dodge.

*   *   *

They rolled onto the Newton Spread just before ten.

Standing on the porch in the shade were two young boys, one with black hair, a few inches taller than the other, who appeared to be the older one. Both were dressed in freshly ironed linen shirts and canvas overalls. Beside them stood a smiling woman in a faded blue calico dress and a crisply starched white apron.

Josh reined up. "Mrs. Newton?"

She nodded at Josh and smiled warmly at Marylee. "You must be the boys' sister. I'd recognize you anywhere," she said, nodding to the boys. "You look just alike."

Tiny dismounted and helped Marylee down. She stepped up on the porch and faced her brothers, both of whom were taller than she. They shifted about nervously, uncertain just what they should do.

She studied them a moment. "You must be Luke," she said to the taller one.

"I'm Simon."

"I'm Luke," announced the other boy.

For several awkward moments, the three just stared at one another.

Josh couldn't help wondering if they were going to stand there all day looking just at one another. At that moment, Mrs. Newton took Marylee by the arm. "Why don't we all go inside to the parlor? It's much cooler than out here on the porch."

Josh and Tiny hung back. "You too, gentlemen," she said.

"No, thank you, ma'am," Josh replied. "Seeing as how this is kind of a family reunion of sorts, we'll just wait out here in the shade of the porch."

Fifteen minutes later, Luke stormed out the door. "I ain't going nowhere," he shouted over his shoulder. "Not until them murdering Comancheros is hung."

Tiny stopped him. "Whoa, there, button. Take it easy. What's going on in there?"

The young boy glared up at him, his eyes blazing defiance. "You can't make me either, so don't try."

"Don't try what, Luke?" asked Josh, who was leaning against the porch post, pulling out a bag of Bull Durham and lazily building a cigarette. "We're not going to try nothing."

The thirteen-year-old shot a blistering look back into the house. "She wants us to leave here with her. I ain't going, and she can't make me. Why, I just barely remember her. I ain't seen her since I was three, and now she comes in here and starts ordering me around." He shook his head. "I'm going to run down them that killed Matt and John if it takes the rest of my life." He glared up at Josh and added, "And that's a promise as sure as I'm standing here."

* * *

Subdued, Marylee remained silent throughout the ride back to Atascocita, shocked that her brothers had refused to accompany her. Neither Josh nor Tiny said a word.

When they reached the livery, Frenchy raised an eyebrow at the empty rear seat. She shook her head slowly. Josh shrugged.

Putting on a bright smile, Frenchy looked up at Marylee. "You must be tired. I just brewed some store tea. It'll refresh you, and you can rest before supper."

With a wan expression, Marylee replied, "Thank you, but I'm not thirsty. I'd just like to lie down for a few minutes if you don't mind."

After the young woman disappeared into the livery office, Frenchy came over to Josh, who was unhitching the team. "Didn't work out, huh?"

"Nope. Boys refused to go with her."

Rubbing the back of her neck, Frenchy muttered, "I could have told her that."

"Maybe so, Frenchy, but she wouldn't have listened. Like I told you before, she's mighty hardheaded. She's got to be pole-axed before she'll believe anything she don't want to believe."

With a wry grin, she slapped the palm of her hand with her quirt. "Some folks are like that."

Tiny swung his saddle up on a saddle rack. "Can't

she get something legal-like that would make the boys go with her? They're underage. She's growed."

Frenchy shrugged. "I don't know if she can or not, but even if she could, I don't think it would do her any good. At least not right now."

Josh hesitated in unsnapping the traces from the bay. "Hold on there, Frenchy. You lost me on that one. What do you mean, at least not right now?"

At that moment, George opened the office door. "Howdy, boys. Any problems?"

"Not a one," Tiny replied.

Josh persisted. "What did you mean, at least not now, Frenchy? Why can't she get a legal order that will force the boys to go on with her to California?"

She pressed her lips together tightly.

George glared at her. "Did you go and open your mouth, old lady?"

She sniffed and jutted out her jaw. "Well, they'll find out about it sooner or later. Might as well tell them now," she snapped back.

Josh glanced at George, then back to Frenchy. "Find out what?"

George shook his head and gave Frenchy a half-hearted wave. "Go ahead and tell 'em."

Frenchy glanced over her shoulder in the direction of the office. "While you all was gone, I happened to run into the banker. According to him, the

Gaston brothers didn't keep none of their money in the bank."

For a moment, Josh didn't comprehend the implication of what she said. Then it hit him. "You mean, she doesn't have any money, any gold?"

Nodding slowly, Frenchy replied, "Only what she's got herself."

Behind Josh, Tiny whistled. "I don't reckon she's going to get as much of them dowries as she thought."

Josh glanced at the closed door behind which Marylee had disappeared. "You tell her?"

Frenchy shook her head. "I don't have the heart. The banker is coming over tomorrow morning."

With a soft whistle, Josh shook his head.

Chapter Seventeen

Next morning while Josh and Tiny unloaded the wagons, a slender man wearing a three-piece suit and a black bowler hat entered the livery office. Moments later, George Buckalew hobbled out, shaking his head.

"Something wrong, George?" Josh asked, rolling a barrel of flour into the corner.

The old man shook his head slowly. "Feel sorry for that little girl. That was Banker McGregor. Frenchy figured he'd be the one to tell her about the money."

Josh nodded. "That's what she said yesterday."

Tiny tossed another hundred pound sack of grain on the waist-high stack he was building, then paused. "You reckon Miss Marylee has got herself enough money to go on to California, Josh?"

"Got no idea," he replied, shaking his head as he tilted another barrel of flour and started rolling it to the corner of the livery. For a fleeting moment, he found himself hoping she didn't have the funds, but then he cursed himself for having such a thought. Never wish hurt on anyone, his Pa had always told him.

Moments later, the office door burst open and Banker McGregor looked out. "Better get in here, George. Miss Gaston just fainted."

After a few minutes, Marylee moaned and slowly opened her eyes. Her face was pale as fresh snow. "I-I'm sorry for causing you so much trouble," she mumbled. "I-I—"

"Hush now, child," cooed Frenchy, who was bathing the young woman's pale cheeks with a damp cloth. "You had a big shock. Just rest there. You'll feel better directly."

The young woman's bottom lip quivered. She closed her eyes tightly, but tears welled from them and ran down the sides of her face. "I can't believe it," she whispered.

Josh shifted his feet, at a loss for words.

Suddenly, Marylee's eyes lit up. "I know what I can do."

Frenchy leaned back. "What's that, child?"

She sat up and smiled broadly at the older woman.

"I can sell the ranch and use that money to get us to California." She nodded emphatically. "That's what I'll do."

Arching an eyebrow, Frenchy laid her hand on Marylee's arm. "What about the boys, Luke and Simon? They'd have to agree to sell out." The young woman frowned at Frenchy, who explained. "If John and Matt didn't leave a will, the ranch belongs to the three of you. And from what you said about the way the boys threw a fit, I got me a feeling they sure won't cotton to going to California or agreeing to sell the ranch."

Marylee's face crumpled into tears. She shook her head. "This is a nightmare, a horrible, horrible nightmare."

A heavy silence fell over the room until two words broke it. "Maybe not."

As one, they all looked around at old George Buckalew.

"What are you talking about, old man?" Frenchy snapped.

He waved a shrunken hand at her. "Hear me out." He shuffled forward and looked down at Marylee. "None of us is thinking straight. There had always been talk that your brothers hid their gold at the ranch. The fact they didn't keep none in the bank sort of backs up that talk. But, it's a fact your brothers had gold. They always paid their bills with gold coins. Each year when they sold off sheep and cows, they insisted on being paid off in gold. Never trusted paper money." He hesitated and glanced sheepishly at Marylee. "I'd wager a tidy sum that the gold was the reason that no-account Comanchero, Archiveque, hit the spread. Now maybe them Comancheros found the gold or maybe they didn't," he added with a smug gleam in his eyes. "Maybe Luke or Simon got an idea where the gold was kept."

Marylee sat upright, her tears drying. "I hadn't thought of that." She swung her legs over the side of the bed. "Let's ask them."

"Hold on, Miss Marylee," said Josh. "Why don't you let me and Tiny ride out to the Newton place." He grinned crookedly. "Save a heap of time not having to rig up the surrey again. We'll be back in a couple hours."

She started to protest, but Frenchy laid a hand on her shoulder. "He's right, child. You just wash those dried tears off your face and before you know it, these two jaspers will be back."

Three hours later, Josh and Tiny rode in followed by Luke and Simon. Frenchy and Marylee met them in the livery. "What are you boys doing here? I didn't think you—I mean—"

Luke explained. "Simon and me still feel the same way about California, but we're family, and we want to find the gold as much as you do."

A frown knit her tiny forehead as she stared at the boys in disbelief. "You mean, you don't know where John and Matt hid the gold?"

The older of the boys, Luke, shook his head. "No, but we don't think they hid it in the house. We got us an idea where it might be." He looked around at his brother, who nodded his agreement.

"Luke's right, Marylee," Simon explained, the timbre of his high-pitched voice breaking. "The ranch is full of caves. Why, there's caves everywhere. It might take some doing, but I bet we can find it."

"Yeah," Luke chimed in. His face grew hard. "But even if we do, we still ain't going to California." He glared at his sister defiantly.

She eyed him imperiously. "We'll see when the time comes."

"No, we won't." Luke shook his head emphatically. "If you don't want to come out to the ranch and help us find the gold, we'll do it ourselves."

"And when we do," Simon added, "we'll give you your share and you can go on to California, but Luke and me, we're going to make a go of the ranch. After all, that's where Matt and John are buried."

Josh suppressed a grin as she glared up at her brothers. Finally, he spoke up. "The boys have a good idea, Miss Marylee. Go out to the ranch with them while they search. Who knows what might come about? At least this way, you'd get to know your brothers, and they'd get to know you. Never can tell what might come of that."

"He's right, child," said Frenchy.

Marylee stared at the two boys for several seconds, then shrugged and shook her head. "Well, then, I guess that's all I can ask for." She paused and added, "And while we're there, we'll see if we can find their will."

Luke and Simon grinned broadly at each other.

Frenchy slapped her quirt against her leg. "Well, then, what are we waiting for? Josh, you and Tiny hitch up the mules. Carry that load of supplies out to the Gaston spread. They got to have something to live on. If you hurry it up, you can get there before dark."

Marylee started to protest. "But, I don't have the money to pay you for the goods. I—"

"Hush now," Frenchy said. "Pay us later." She gestured to Josh and Tiny. With a mischievous twinkle in her eyes, she added, "And while you're at it, keep these two galoots out there with you for a few days. You boys don't mind helping out, do you?"

Josh saw the sly smile on her face and knew she

had deliberately posed the question in front of Marylee so he couldn't refuse. "You're the boss," he replied without enthusiasm.

Frenchy then smiled up at Luke and Simon. "Marylee, you got two fine young men there, but I reckon there's enough work out there for everyone, ain't that right, boys?"

Luke nodded. "Yes, ma'am. Plenty work."

While Tiny and the boys were hitching up the mules, Josh got Frenchy alone in the kitchen. "That was a sneaky trick out there."

She laughed, and her eyes twinkled. She reached up and patted him on a sun-browned cheek. "Reckon it was, but with the feelings you got against her, you wouldn't have gone otherwise. Tiny would have, but you wouldn't." She studied him closely, and then her eyes grew wide. "Would you?"

With a faint grin, the lanky cowpoke cleared his throat. "Oh, I don't know. You might be surprised. I might have," he replied, pondering the same question himself. "Still, I'd have liked to be the one to say yes or no."

The older woman feigned contrition. "I apologize. Next time, I'll give you a choice. All right?"

Josh saw the amusement in her eyes. He chuckled

and shook his head. "No, you won't. You'll do the same thing again just to get your way."

Her only reply was a burst of bright laughter.

He grew serious. "That's decent of you to let them take the supplies. You might have sold them here in town. Wouldn't be a total loss."

The laughter faded from her eyes. "We'll manage. That old man and me, we always manage."

He remembered Tiny's suggestion about the poker winnings. He jammed his hand in his pocket and pulled out the roll of bills. He tossed the roll to Frenchy. "Here. This will help."

She caught the roll in both hands and stared at it. "What's this?"

With a lopsided grin, Josh replied, "Call it thanks for helping me and Tiny out of a bad spot."

She handed the roll back to him. "I can't take this."

Josh backed away. "All right, then say we just bought ourselves two hundred and fifty dollars worth of Buckalew Livery and Freight. Once you're back on your feet and want to buy us out, we'll take it."

The older woman's bottom lip quivered and tears welled in her eyes. She threw her arms around Josh's neck and hugged him. "You're a good boy."

Tentatively, Josh put his arms around her and gently hugged her in return.

She whispered against his chest, "Never can tell. You might come to learn that little girl ain't as stuck-up as you figure."

Cullen Leach frowned when he saw Josh climb up on the loaded freight wagon and head south, accompanied by the Gaston woman, her young brothers, and the big jasper who worked for Frenchy Buckalew. He ran his fingers through his thinning hair.

What the Sam Hill were they up to? There could be only one reason they were heading back to the ranch with a load of supplies. Frustration washed over him, and he clamped down on his cigar so hard he bit it in two.

The road to the Gaston spread led across the rolling prairie, forded the Canadian River, and climbed back up on the caprock. An hour later, Luke pulled up alongside the wagon. "Won't be long now."

Josh nodded. "You run sheep out on your spread, I hear."

The young boy nodded. "About eight hundred head. And I reckon about a couple hundred or so cows. And more chickens and guineas than you can shake a stick at."

"You boys look after the stock yourself?"

A grin played over his square face. "We look after the cows, but we have three *pastores* tending the sheep."

"*Pastores?*"

"Sheepherders. Mexicans. They live with the herds, move about with them."

"You have any ranch hands?"

"No. Matt, he was the oldest, well, he figured the four of us could handle what stock we had without help. And the times we needed extra, Matt would hire them in town."

Josh gazed around the flat tableland surrounding them. "I figure you'd have to have a mighty large spread to graze a couple hundred head of cows. From the looks of the grass around here, you'd need two hundred acres just for one head."

Luke laughed. "Up here, yeah, but we're down in a valley with three year-round creeks running through the place. Just wait. You'll see. It's mighty pretty. Good graze." He looked around and pointed to the southeast. "There. See that needle peak. Our spread is just south of it." He glanced at the sun dropping in the west. "We ought to get there just about sundown."

Fifteen minutes later, they pulled up on the rim of the caprock. Josh caught his breath when he saw the lush valley a hundred feet below. A small mesa sat in the middle of the valley and in front of it, shaded by tall cottonwoods, were two rectangular buildings facing each other across a strip of hardpan.

Josh whistled softly. "I see what you mean, son. I don't blame you. I wouldn't want to leave this place either."

Clucking chickens and squawking guineas scattered in all directions when Josh reined the team up at the hitching rail in front of the adobe and rock building with a parapet around the perimeter of the flat roof. "Looks like a fort," he muttered, studying the sturdy building.

"That's how we built it. Whenever there's Injun trouble, we'd hold them off from up there," said Simon, pointing to the roof.

Luke reined up. "You didn't help none, Simon. You was too small."

Simon glared at his older brother. "I did so. You take that back."

Ignoring his brother's challenge, Luke jumped off his gray pony and hurried inside. "I'll light the lanterns. Simon can show you where to put the mules for the night. There's feed for them over there."

The interior of the adobe was in shambles. Furniture overturned, drawers emptied, paper strewn everywhere. "Looking for the money, I suspect," muttered Luke, his fists clenched as he went into the bedroom. "They sure tore the place apart."

"I'd like to get my hands on them," Simon growled, his voice breaking.

Luke called through the doorway. "They didn't find the cellar."

He was standing next to an open trapdoor leading into the cellar below. "John and Matt built it for storage and in case of tornadoes."

Josh frowned. "What's down there, Luke?"

"A bunch of stuff," Simon replied. "Grub, guns, ammunition."

"How do you know they didn't find it?" Marylee peered down into the dark hole.

The young boy pointed to an armoire. "The armoire was over it, and besides, look." Dropping to his knees, he lowered a lantern down the opening. The dim light revealed undisturbed shelves filled with an assortment of food and boxes of ammunition and a dozen or so rifles. "If them scavengers had found it, they would have taken the rifles and ammunition."

Josh stepped back and closed the trapdoor. "That's one good thing in our favor."

Marylee released a long sigh and looked over the ruins about her, distressed at the destruction.

"Don't worry none," Josh said, setting a straight-back chair upright. "It'll straighten up. Right now, let's rig up some sleeping arrangements. Tiny and me'll throw our soogans on the kitchen floor."

From far up on the rim of the Staked Plains, a solitary figure watched the activity below until all he could see were the yellow windows punching holes in the dark night. He grunted to himself. Archiveque would be pleased to hear some of the family had returned. Maybe they knew the location of the hidden gold.

Reining his pony to leave, Valdez hesitated, spotting a tiny light flickering below near the main house. In the next second, the light vanished.

At that moment, a full moon eased from behind a line of clouds on the eastern horizon, bathing the countryside in a cold white light.

Down below, Josh squinted at the rim.

Tiny looked in the direction Josh was staring. "What are you looking at?"

"Not sure," he replied, his cigarette dangling from his lips. "I thought I saw moonlight reflect off something up there on the rim."

"Aw, just your imagination."

"Could be, but keep your six-gun by your head tonight."

Tiny grinned. "Always do."

Chapter Eighteen

That the ranch had been well maintained was obvious. The walls inside the main house had been whitewashed, giving the rooms a more expansive feeling. The furniture was rough, but solid.

A wood-burning stove sat against one wall of the kitchen. Fixed beneath the window on the adjacent wall was a small cabinet, in the middle of which was a sink with a hand pump. A rough-hewn, scarred sawbuck table took up the middle of the room.

Josh reckoned the main house was snug in the winter for right now, in the middle of the summer, it was cool and comfortable.

He nodded appreciatively at what he had seen, at the same time wondering just how Marylee would accommodate herself to the surroundings.

This wasn't Philadelphia.

The next morning while they were having their coffee and fried bacon, Josh suggested they unload the wagon and take care of chores around the ranch before setting out to look for the cache of gold coins. "The killers searched the house and the barns. If, like you say, you don't think your brothers kept the gold in here, then wherever the coins are, they'll keep until we get things straightened up around here. Besides, I've got to take the team back to Frenchy today. I'll be back by noon."

The next few days were a whirlwind of work: straightening rooms, repairing furniture, tending stock, seeing after the *pastores* and sheep, and the everyday routine of mending equipment.

Marylee went through every scrap of paper in the house, looked behind every picture, thumbed through every book, turned every piece of clothing inside out, but to her dismay, discovered no will.

From time to time, Josh glanced at the rim of the caprock, remembering the flash of light he had seen that first night. He saw nothing. To his surprise, Marylee did her share without complaining, taking over running the house and the preparation of their meals.

Josh began to think that maybe he was wrong about her. He hoped so, but only three or four days didn't prove anything. A western woman had to possess the staying power of a draft horse, the determination of a mule, and the patience of a saint.

Around the supper table on the fourth night, Luke looked up from his plate of beans. "When do you and Tiny have to go back to Atascocita, Josh?"

Josh sensed a hint of concern in the young boy's voice. With a grin, he joked, "Hadn't thought much about it." He nodded to Marylee, who was sitting across the table from him, and grinned. "Kinda hate to leave all this good grub behind."

"Don't be silly," Marylee said, a tinge of blush creeping up her neck. "But you have to admit," she added, looking around the table at all of them, "I didn't burn the biscuits tonight."

They all laughed. Josh grew serious. "To tell the truth, Luke, Tiny and me talked about it. We reckoned we might stay on awhile, if you folks got no objection."

Tiny nodded emphatically. "We don't want no pay." He jabbed his fork at his cup of coffee. "Just coffee and beans."

Simon grinned. "We hoped you would, even Marylee here."

Her cheeks turned crimson. "Now you hush, Simon Ray. You know better than that. All I said was it was comforting to have Josh and Tiny around."

Luke winked at Josh, who, to his own surprise, realized her words stirred something in him he didn't quite understand.

Simon leaned forward. "So, does that mean we can start looking for the gold tomorrow?"

Josh looked at Marylee. "Things are in good shape around here. I reckon we could spare a couple hands."

Luke slapped his brother on the shoulder. "Let's get to bed so we can get up early."

"Hold on," Josh said. "I figure either me or Tiny needs to go with one of you boys." Before they could protest, he explained. "Take turns. One go one day, one the other. Luke and Tiny can go tomorrow, me and Simon the next day."

"Josh is right, boys," Marylee said. "It won't hurt to have a grown man with you just in case."

"We can take care of ourselves," Luke said defensively.

Josh decided to share his concerns. "I know you can, but think about this, boys. Whoever killed your brothers might still be out there." He gestured in the direction of the caprock rim. "Those kind have no conscience, no qualms about killing anybody. You know that as well as me."

Simon shrugged. "He's right, Luke. Maybe that's the smartest thing to do."

Reluctantly, Luke agreed.

Mad Tom Gristy held the batwing doors open and looked around the saloon, spotting Dave Rynning sitting at a back table with a bottle of whiskey and playing solitaire.

Rynning arched a quizzical eyebrow when the big-bellied man approached.

"Mr. Leach wants us."

Rynning blew softly through his lips and rolled his eyes. "What about?"

Mad Tom shrugged. "He didn't say. He just said for me to find you and bring you back with me. He's mad about something."

The hired killer pushed back from the table. With a sarcastic sneer on his thin lips, he muttered, "Well, let's don't keep the big man waiting."

"That Gaston girl and them two boys are going to try to make a go of that ranch out there," Leach announced from behind his desk, his round face flushed with anger.

Rynning shrugged. "I don't see what the worry is. A woman and two kids? They ain't going to make it."

Leach yanked his cigar from between his thick lips and jabbed it at Rynning. "I've waited long enough for that place. I'm paying you to see they don't make a go of it, you hear?"

His icy eyes mere slits, Rynning nodded. "Don't worry, Mr. Leach. You got nothing to worry about."

"Them two jaspers Frenchy hired must still be out there. I haven't seen them around town. Run them off, and the woman and brats will follow, but I don't want the woman or kids hurt."

Mad Tom leered, revealing gaps between his rotted teeth. "What if them two *hombres* push it?"

Leach shrugged. "Do what you got to do to defend yourself against them."

With saddlebags bulging with biscuits and fried bacon, Tiny and Luke rode out before sunrise heading southeast.

"Just be back before dark," Marylee cautioned her brother.

Tiny winked at Josh. "Cross your fingers for us."

"Keep your eyes open. If the killers didn't find the gold coins, you can bet they'll be keeping a close eye on us just in case we do."

After the dust settled behind Tiny and Luke, Josh and Simon followed Marylee into the kitchen where she poured them a cup of coffee. Marylee slipped onto the table bench and looked at her brother. "Where's Luke going to look today, Simon?"

The young boy poured his coffee in a saucer, which he then picked up with his fingertips and blew on it to cool the steaming black liquid. "Luke and me talked about it last night. We figured our best chance was about a mile south where the caprock turns back into the valley like a finger. It's full of caves."

"What makes him think that's where your brothers might have hidden the gold?"

Slurping on his coffee, Simon knit his brow in concentration. "Well, that's the direction John and Matt would take. Sometimes when they came back with some gold coins, they'd only be gone an hour or so. We figured it took them about fifteen minutes to go in the cave and come out with the gold. That meant the cave was probably about twenty minutes away. That's about how far those caves are."

Nodding to the north, Josh said, "What about the mesa out back here? I saw it's got a heap of caves."

The young boy grinned. "It sure does. That's where Luke and me used to play when we were children, but some of them, you got to be careful of."

Marylee frowned. "Careful? Why?"

He shrugged nonchalantly. "There's dropoffs."

"Dropoffs?"

"Yep. Some got no bottom. At least, Luke and me couldn't hear the rocks we tossed in hit bottom."

Marylee shivered. "I hate caves."

Simon pushed his empty cup away. "Reckon I'll get started feeding the horses." He reached for his hat.

"While you're out there, feed the chickens and bring in the eggs," Marylee said. Before Simon could protest, she added, "I thought I'd bake some pies today if I had the eggs."

Her proposal effectively stifled the young boy's protest. When she looked back around, she saw the look of surprise on Josh's face. She arched an eyebrow and smiled. "When I lived in Missouri, my mother taught me to cook. It's all coming back to me. I can still bake a pie that will make your mouth water."

At a loss for words, Josh nodded.

Marylee grew serious. "Do you really believe that whoever killed Matt and John didn't find the gold, that it's still somewhere around?"

Josh shrugged, relieved to be back on a subject with which he was comfortable. "I figure the odds are in your favor, Miss Marylee."

She drew a deep breath. "I hope you're right."

Josh leaned back and stared at her for several seconds.

She shifted uncomfortably under his gaze. "Is something wrong?"

With a grin, he replied, "I just can't believe you're the same lady who rode down here from Dodge City with us."

Eyeing him shrewdly, she answered, "Oh? And why is that?" There was a wariness in her tone.

Immediately, Josh wished he had not made the observation, for he didn't know exactly how to explain what he meant. "It's just that, well, on the trail, things bothered you, but here—why, you're letting all the hardships sort of roll off your back like water off a duck."

She arched an eyebrow. "Well, I'm going to disappoint you, I'm afraid, but I haven't changed. Not really."

Puzzled, Josh gestured to the kitchen. "But all this, the ranch, the cooking—you took right to it."

"Survival, Mr. Carson. One thing I remember from my father is you have to go along with whatever happens if you want to survive. I'm not so foolish that I don't realize that if I do my part, if I carry my weight, we'll find the gold coins sooner, and that means, despite the fact that Matt and John obviously left no will, I can get out of here sooner. Besides, once my brothers get to know me better, then I can talk them into leaving this forsaken country with me."

Josh studied her a moment. He had been wrong. She had not changed. She was still the same self-centered, selfish woman who had ridden down to Atascocita with them. He nodded somberly and reached for his hat. "I think I'll give Simon a hand with the stock."

As Josh crossed the hardpan to the barn, he glanced at the caprock rim just in time to see the morning sunlight flash off a piece of metal.

Chapter Nineteen

Up on the rim, Diego Valdez rested in the shade of his scrubby horse, a spavined sorrel he had stolen from a drunk Mexican in Hidetown. He chewed on a strip of jerky and waited.

Two had ridden out from the ranch below. He must wait until they returned to learn of their fortune.

The day was as those before, hot and dry, and to add to Valdez's discomfort, an afternoon rainstorm swept through, soaking him.

Just before dusk, the two returned.

Mounting, he eased his pony down the steep slope to the valley below and headed for the main house to spy on the *gringos*.

* * *

189

Luke and Tiny had ridden in with a look of disgust on their faces. "At the tenth cave, we found where the gold had been hidden, but it was all gone except this one," Luke said, flipping a gold Double Eagle on the table.

Tiny nodded. "There was a hole dug in the wall, but like the boy said, that was all that was left."

Marylee's face crumpled with disappointment. "Then the Comancheros found it?"

Josh remembered the reflection of light on the caprock. He had a gut feeling the gold was still around. "We can't be certain. Maybe your brothers moved it."

Simon frowned. "Why would they do that?"

"Closer to the house maybe. A number of reasons."

Later that night, Diego Valdez rode into a camp hidden in a deep gully on the caprock that carried runoff rainwater to the valley. Sleeping Comancheros wrapped in their blankets were scattered about. He walked directly to a tall, imposing Mexican standing in front of the fire.

Tearing off a chunk of broiled beef with his teeth, Sosthenes Archiveque eyed the smaller man with disdain. "Well?"

Valdez nodded. "*Sí*. As you thought, *Patron*. They look for the gold. Two ride out this morning. They go to caves. They find only one coin."

Archiveque wiped his greasy fingers on the stained shirt stretched across his barrel-sized belly. "You are sure?"

"*Sí.* I listen at the window. That is all they find."

The Comanchero leader arched an eyebrow. "That is what they say. Perhaps they know we watch." He eyed Diego suspiciously. "Maybe they say more."

"No, *Patron.* Diego, he tells the truth. Only one coin."

Archiveque slowly nodded. "*Bueno.* Eat, sleep, return tomorrow."

The next morning, Josh looked up from his breakfast of fried bacon, hen eggs, and biscuits. "We had a visitor last night."

The others looked at him, puzzled.

"A visitor? What do you mean, partner," asked Tiny.

"Outside the window over the sink. Boot heels. Someone was at the window last night."

"I was out there yesterday afternoon," Simon offered. "I reckon they're probably mine."

Josh arched an eyebrow. "Before or after the rain?"

"Before."

The lanky cowpoke shook his head. "Weren't yours, then. These are sharp and crisp, made after the rain passed through." He hesitated, then added, "Our first night back, I thought I spotted something or someone up on the caprock rim. Yesterday, the sun flashed off something shiny up there. It might have been just ground minerals. I don't know, but I figure I'll ride up there today and see what I can find."

A worried look came over Marylee. "Do you really think that's what it was, ground minerals?"

He studied her a moment. "No. And I think it answers the question about the gold."

She frowned. "What was that?"

"If it had been found or just moved." He continued, "Those footprints are pretty solid proof that the killers didn't find the gold. Why else would they be snooping about?"

Marylee nodded slowly. "I see."

"And if they didn't take it, then your brothers moved it."

"Yeah," Luke exclaimed, his youthful face lighting with excitement. "That's why they're snooping around. They want to know if we found it."

With a gleeful smile on her face, Marylee leaned over and squeezed Simon's arm. "It's still out there. Isn't that wonderful. It's still out there."

Simon laughed. "I knew it was. I knew it was."

Josh's next words crushed their glee. "We haven't found it yet, and before you get too excited over the prospect, you best remember, those Comancheros will be coming back. If one was listening last night, they know we found one coin. They killed once for the gold. They'll kill again."

His words sobered them. Marylee's face paled. "What are we going to do?"

Tiny cleared his throat. "Nothing."

They all looked around at him in surprise.

The big man shrugged his massive shoulders and explained. "We just go about the ranching business like that's all we had in mind."

Josh understood what his partner meant. "Tiny's right. We don't make anymore deliberate searches for the cache of gold coins. Instead, we ride out to check the herd, visit with the *pastores,* inspect the creeks. They know we only found one coin. We'll make them think we've given up on the gold."

Luke's face lit. "And while we're doing that, we can still look for it."

"Except," Josh added, "it won't look like we're searching for it." He turned to Simon. "Do you put the guineas up at night with the chickens?"

The young boy nodded. "Coyotes'll get them if we don't."

"Well, why don't we start leaving a few of those little guinea hens out. Take a chance on the coyotes. When I was a kid, guineas were our watchdogs."

Simon grinned. "All right. I'll build a roost on top of the house today."

Tiny rose from the table and reached for his Stetson hanging on a peg in the wall. "You want me to ride up to the rim with you?"

Josh downed the last of his coffee, and dumped his dishes in the boiling water in the wreck pan on the stove. "No. You and the boys take care of chores around here. I'll be back by noon or thereabouts."

Planting his hands on his saddle horn, Mad Tom stood in his stirrups and peered down into the valley as Josh rode out of the barn and headed for the caprock north of the main house. Wheeling his pony about, he dug his spurs into the animal's flanks and headed for town like a coyote for a henhouse.

Diego Valdez saw the rider leave the ranch and head directly toward him. With a sly grin, he glanced at the hooves on his sorrel. He had the cunning to wrap them with flour sacks, especially after the rain yesterday.

Rising from where he had been sitting, he swung into the saddle. The *gringo* would find nothing, but with Valdez's surveillance of the ranch being discovered the Comanchero knew he had to find a new hideout from which he could spy on the ranch, and he knew the perfect place.

He guided his pony over a vein of rocky plate and

down into a wash a half-mile distant. There, at a wet-weather waterhole, he lost his trail among the muddy tracks of wild cattle and then followed the labyrinth of gullies and washes into a cave below the rim of the caprock.

Josh studied the ground on the caprock, spotting no fresh tracks, only smudges on the ground. He grinned, realizing what the jasper had done. It was an old trick, an effective one.

Leaning down from his saddle, the lanky cowpoke followed the faint marks until he reached the vein of rock plates. He grunted with resignation. The faint trail had vanished. He clicked his tongue and sent his pony trotting along the plate in the same direction until he reached the wash.

As he rounded a bend in the wash, a half a dozen wild longhorns bellowed and scattered, slinging mud with their hooves as they dashed up the wash to a fork where the animals split in two directions.

Josh reined up his pony "Whoa, boy. Here's as far as we go. We won't find anything up there except long-horn sign." He reined his dun around, then hesitated, suddenly curious as to just where the washes led.

He glanced at the sun. Mid-morning. He had time to do a little exploring. Never can tell, he told him-self. Might come in handy.

Josh headed up the wash. His eyes narrowed when he spotted horse sign among the longhorn tracks. The wash forked several times, but Josh stayed with the sign. Suddenly, he picked up the sharp smell of burning sage. Reining up, he remained motionless in the saddle, his ears straining for the slightest sound, but all he heard was the chirruping of crickets.

The acrid smell of the wood smoke remained strong as he pushed up the wash. Ahead, the wash forked, and the tracks he had been following led up the right branch. He ground-reined his dun and eased forward on foot. As he drew near the bend in the gully, voices reached his ears.

The lanky cowpoke froze, then slipped the rawhide loop off the hammer of his .44 Colt. Removing his hat, he pressed up against the wall of the gully and peered around the corner.

Nothing. The wash cut sharply back to the left. The voices came from behind that bend. Dropping into a crouch, Josh darted across the sandy bed and pressed up against the side of the gully. Peering around the bend, his blood ran cold. A dozen Comancheros lounged around a blazing fire over which a hindquarter of beef roasted on a spit. Behind the spit were several wagons, celerities, and army ambulances.

He jerked his head back and leaned against the

side of the gully, his brain racing. This had to be a temporary camp of the band that killed Matt and John, the one led by Sosthenes Archiveque. Part him wanted to spy on them, to see if he could spot the leader, but wisdom urged him back to his pony.

At least, he told himself as he backtracked out of the wash, there was no question the gold remained hidden, but just as certain was the fact that sooner or later, they would have to deal with the Comancheros, and their cruel leader, Sosthenes Archiveque.

Just before Josh reached the water hole, he heard voices from ahead. Quickly, he backed his dun around a fork off the main wash and waited, shucking his six-gun just in case the riders came down his wash.

"Blast it, you should have followed him and then come and got me. No telling where he is now."

Josh stiffened. He recognized the voice of Dave Rynning from the saloon that first day in town.

The guttural voice of Mad Tom Gristy replied, "I figured it was smarter to have two of us."

Rynning sneered. "I tell you what it was. You didn't want to face that jasper all by your lonesome. That's what it was."

"Naw. That ain't it. I could take him. I just figured between the two of us, we wouldn't have no trouble planting that saddle tramp like a potato. Soon as we do that, we get the big one down at the ranch, and then that little gal and them two brats will lose no time in lighting a shuck out of this part of the country. That's why."

"Yeah." Rynning sneered. "I'm sure that's why."

Suddenly, a devious idea hit Josh.

He dug his heels into his pony and shot forward and headed back in the direction of the Comancheros, hoping to draw the two gunnies after him.

Behind him he heard Mad Tom shout. "There he is."

Leaning over the neck of his pony, Josh muttered a hasty prayer that his pony wouldn't stumble.

A shot rang out, and a chunk of soil exploded from the side of the gully ahead of him. Leaning to his right, Josh whipped around a bend.

Two more shots echoed down the gully, and something tugged at his sleeve, burning his arm.

Just before he reached the last bend before the fork leading to the Comanchero camp, he wheeled about and touched off two quick shots, causing Rynning and Mad Tom to yank their ponies around.

By the time they calmed their horses, Josh had disappeared.

Rynning cursed and dug his Mexican spurs into his horse's flanks. The searing pain drove the frightened animal into an all-out gallop.

Josh rounded the last bend and sent his dun up the

left fork instead of the right, hoping the two gunnies would follow the plethora of tracks into the other. Around the first bend, he reined up, his six-gun in his hand, cocked and ready just in case they took the wrong fork and ran upon him.

They didn't.

When Mad Tom and Rynning rounded the last bend, they found themselves facing a dozen armed Comancheros who immediately started firing at them. "What the—" shouted Rynning, yanking his pony around and trying to retreat.

Mad Tom screamed as a slug tore into his left arm.

Suddenly Sosthenes Archiveque's voice bellowed out. *"La parada disparando, los hombres! Estos son nuestros amigos! Ellos significan no daño!"* "Stop shooting, men. These are our friends. They mean us no harm."

Josh didn't hear Archiveque's shouted command for he was already halfway back to the water hole.

Chapter Twenty

Cullen Leach glared at his two hired guns, ignoring the bandage on Mad Tom's arm. "You had him, and you let him get away." He slammed his fist on the desk. "What the blazes do I pay you for?"

"But, Mr. Leach," whined Mad Tom. "It wasn't our fault. We just took the wrong turn, or we would've got him."

The corpulent businessman cursed. "Stop making excuses. I pay you for results, and I expect results." He studied the two with contempt. "What's Archiveque doing in this part of the country? After he took care of the Gaston brothers, I reckoned he'd light out of here faster'n a cat with its tail on fire."

Rynning arched an eyebrow. "He never found all

the gold that them brothers hid. He found a couple hundred at the house, but that was all."

Leach had heard the story of the Gaston gold ever since the brothers settled in eight years earlier, but he figured it had been told so much that it had grown out of proportion. He grunted. "There might be some gold hid out there, but it probably ain't enough to be worth looking for." He paused and retrieved a cigar from the humidor on his desk. After clipping the end, he touched a match to it and blew a steam of blue smoke into the air. "Tell you what. Find Archiveque and see how much he wants to join up with me in running those jaspers off the ranch. Remind him that my money is a sure bet. The gold ain't. But like I told him before, if there is gold there, he can have it."

The supper table grew somber that night as Josh related the events of the morning. "So," he added. "It looks to me like we're up against Cullen Leach and now this band of cutthroat Comancheros led by that Archiveque *hombre*."

Tiny, who usually put away a double helping of every dish on the table, toyed with his half-eaten bowl of beef stew. "Well, partner, I don't reckon those jaspers have given us a much of a choice. We can't run. We got to stay here."

A frown knit Marylee's forehead. "But why would Mr. Leach want to drive us away? We've never done anything to him."

Josh grunted. He'd seen it before. "Power. According to Frenchy, Leach is trying to run them out of business. We're pretty certain that one of Leach's gunnies named Crawford was one of the bushwhackers that jumped us when we came off the caprock. Leach is one of those who wants the whole country." He hooked his thumb over his shoulder. "After all, you folks have the choice land around here, a hundred sections with running creeks, good grass, and the caprock a built-in windbreak against winter cold. *Hombres* out here have been known to kill for a lot less."

That night, Josh and Tiny inventoried the weapons and ammunition down in the cellar. Tiny held up a Winchester .66. "Blazes, Josh. There's enough firepower here to hold off an army. Maybe we ought to just sit tight."

"You mean hole up in here, in the house?"

Tiny shrugged. "We could. We got enough grub for a month."

With a faint grin, Josh agreed. "What then? What if we do just that, and they outwait us?" When Tiny didn't reply, Josh added. "No, partner. I think we've got to take it to them. If we can cut off the head of the snake, the body will die."

Replacing the Winchester on the shelf, Tiny grunted. "Which snake you talking about, Archiveque or Leach?"

Josh didn't answer. He was busy studying the rock walls of the cellar.

"Did you hear me?"

He ignored Tiny's question. "You notice these walls?"

"Huh?" The big man frowned and glanced at the walls of flat rock stacked on each other and the cracks filled in with adobe and then whitewashed. "What about them? They're just rock. What's so important about that?"

A nebulous thought crept into Josh's head, but he couldn't quite pin it down. "I wonder why the brothers didn't settle for dirt walls. That's all that's in most cellars."

Tiny rolled his eyes. "How should I know? Maybe they was just partial to rocks. What difference does it make?"

Josh glanced at his partner. "None, I don't reckon." He grinned. "Now what was you saying?"

Impatiently Tiny replied, "I said, which snake was you talking about, Archiveque or Leach?"

Josh climbed out of the cellar and looked back down as Tiny clambered up the ladder. "Both."

Suddenly the guineas outside raised a racket.

Shucking his six-gun, Josh dashed for the front door, but by the time he had it open, the sound of racing hoofbeats behind the main house echoed across the valley.

With Tiny right on his heels, Josh slid to a halt at the corner of the house. In the dim starlight, he could make out a single rider heading for the caprock.

Back inside, Marylee was waiting. "Did you see them?"

"Him," Josh replied. "Just one. Not enough light to make him out, but I'll wager it was one of Archiveque's Comancheros."

"Yeah," growled Tiny.

Simon interrupted. "Those guineas sure did a dandy job warning us, didn't they, Josh?"

He grinned at the boy. "A right dandy job, Simon." He hesitated as a scheming thought hit him. "Simon, didn't you tell us that some of the caves in the mesa had dropoffs?"

The young boy nodded, a puzzled frown on his face. "Yes, sir." He glanced at his brother and shrugged.

"Tomorrow, I want you boys to show me, all right?"

Simon nodded. "Sure, but why?"

Josh grinned at Tiny. "We know they're watching us. So, let's give them something to watch. Maybe we can start at the tail of the snake first. Put a scare into that jasper on the rim, and maybe word will spread."

Tiny frowned. "Scare? What do you mean?"

Josh grinned. "Here's what I got in mind."

The next morning, Diego Valdez watched curiously as a man and boy entered the mouth of a cave in the mesa behind the main house. Sometime later, they rushed out and raced to the house. Moments later, the whole family of *gringos* ran back to the cave. When they emerged a few minutes later, they were laughing.

The Comanchero stroked the thin beard on his chin. He considered relaying the information to Sosthenes Archiveque, but then considered that if that cave contained the gold coins, and if he were to find them that night, he could be halfway to Mexico before he was missed.

Before the moon rose that night, Valdez came around the mesa from the south, taking care to stay far enough away from the main house so he wouldn't disturb those worrisome *guinea gallinas*.

Leaving his spavined horse, he slipped the last few yards to the cave and stepped out of the starlight into the dark. He struck a lucifer and spotted a lantern on the floor. Lighting it, he held it in front of him as he made his way into the cave. Suddenly, he jerked to a halt, staring at a yawning hole in the floor, stretching from wall to wall.

A sharp voice from behind froze him. "Don't move a muscle, *amigo. Dispararé!* I will shoot. Now, turn around, real slow."

The Comanchero turned and stared into the muzzles of two six-guns. He whined. "Please, *señors.* I mean no harm. I just look for a safe place to spend the night."

A sneer curled Josh's lips. "*Usted miente!*"

Valdez shook his head and glanced over his shoulder at the hole behind him. "No, *señor.* Valdez, he do not lie."

Tiny cocked his .44 Remington. "I think we just ought to shoot this Mexican and kick him in the hole. No one will ever find him. Nobody's never found the others," he added, doing his utmost to suppress a grin.

Josh stared at Valdez with eyes of ice. "We know you ride with Archiveque the Comanchero. We know you spy on us."

"*Sí, señor,* but Archiveque, he make me. Back in

Coahuila, he holds my wife and children as prison-
ers. He will kill them if I do not do as he says.
Please, *señor.* Do not shoot me. I will leave
Archiveque." He dropped his head to his chest. "*Por
favor.* I beg of you."

"I don't believe you, *amigo.* If we turn you loose,
you'll head straight back to Archiveque." Josh shook
his head. "No, I think we need to show just how serious we are." He nodded to the hole behind Valdez.
"We're going to string a rope around your feet and
drop you down in that hole for a few minutes. Maybe
that will convince you."

"I'll get the horse and rope," Tiny said, backing
away a step and then leaving the cave. Once outside,
he chuckled, figuring they'd scared the Comanchero
enough that he would never return to Archiveque.

With the big *gringo* gone, Diego Valdez saw his
chance. He hurled the lantern at Josh and grabbed for
his six-gun, but he took a backward step, and found
nothing but air.

The lantern hit the rocky floor and exploded,
spreading burning coal oil from wall to wall. Josh
leaped back, too busy slapping at the flames licking
at his legs to pay any attention to Valdez' dying
scream.

Tiny rushed in. "What the Sam Hill—where is he?

What happened?" Then he realized what had taken place. "You mean, he fell—"

Josh nodded. "Pulled his hogleg. He should have just stood still, but he didn't."

Tiny shivered. "Rough way to go."

Outside, Josh tied the reins of Valdez' horse around the saddle horn and gave the animal a slap on the rump.

"Archiveque's going to wonder what happened to his man."

Josh grinned. "Let him wonder."

Chapter Twenty-one

Archiveque scratched his head as he stared at Valdez's spavined sorrel. "Where you find *el caballo,* did you say?"

The Comanchero nodded to the west. "That way. Something must have happened to Diego, *Patron.* He not be thrown. He *bueno* rider."

The big-bellied Comanchero shook his head slowly, his black eyes fixed on the sorrel. "*Sí.* You are right." His gaze swept from the horse in the direction of the ranch. With a malevolent glare, he said. "I know who did this thing to Diego." He spat on the fire. "And they will pay. *En el nombre de Dios,* they will pay. I will take a boy, and they will pay for his return with the gold, or else he will join Valdez."

* * *

Tiny and Luke rode in mid-morning and announced that a large number of beeves had drifted up on the caprock. "We would have run them back," said Tiny, dismounting and picking up his blood bay's front hoof, "but my horse came up lame."

"I don't know why them ornery cows would do something dumb like that." Luke fussed from his saddle. "The graze up there ain't near as good as it is down here."

Josh slapped him on the leg. "Only thing dumber than some horses is cows. You two light. Simon and me'll herd 'em back. I think your sister baked up some mock apple pie this morning."

There was no breeze, and the sun blazed down on the valley. Heat rose from the ground in waves that distorted distant objects, reminding Josh of the mirrors in the Fun House at the circus over in Fort Worth the year before.

Around noon, they picked up the trail, and as they followed it, Josh began noticing shod tracks among those of the cows. The hair on the back of his neck bristled. The cows had not drifted. They were driven. He cursed under his breath. First Leach, then Archiveque, and now rustlers.

The sign was clear as fresh spring water. It appeared to Josh that the trail led to Rica Creek near the bottom of the caprock and then upward.

"There," shouted Simon, pointing to the caprock. "Up there."

Looking in the direction the boy was pointing, Josh spotted several head of beeves grazing on the rim. He hesitated. That didn't make sense. Rustlers wouldn't have left any stock behind, and the cows weren't so dumb they'd leave lush graze for bad. "Well, boy. Let's get them. But, let's go careful-like." They kicked their ponies into a canter.

Sweat soaked Josh's shirt and burned his eyes. He eyed the welcome shade of the cottonwoods and willows lining Rica Creek. Once they pushed the cows down off the caprock, they might just stop and rest a bit. Maybe even take a dip in the cool waters of the bubbling creek.

At the creek's edge, Josh's dun stumbled in the mud, and a powerful blow slammed into his skull, knocking him backward over the rump of his pony and sending him sprawling into the shallow creek.

Simon jerked around at the roar of the rifle just in time to see Josh go down. "Josh!" Before he could rein around, three Comancheros burst from the cottonwoods and willows and surrounded him.

Archiveque rode into the creek slowly and stared

down at the motionless body in the shallow water, which by now was running red with blood. He grunted. "When they find the body, they will know Archiveque is not one to be taken lightly."

From somewhere beyond the blackness surrounding him, Josh heard voices. Slowly they came closer.

"He's waking up," whispered a woman's voice.

"Yeah. I always told him he was hard-headed," said a voice he recognized as his partner's.

She bathed Josh's angular face with cool water. "I hope he knows what happened to Simon."

"I told you, Miss Marylee," said Tiny. "From the sign on the shore, somebody's done taken the youngster."

Luke spoke up. "But why?"

"It's got to be the gold. I don't know what else it could be."

Josh moaned and slowly opened his eyes. His head pounded like someone was banging it with a twelve-pound blacksmith's hammer. He tried to sit, but Marylee stayed him with a tiny hand. "Don't. Not yet. Just lay there."

"Yeah, partner," growled Tiny. "Get the cobwebs out of your head."

"Luke," whispered Marylee. "Get Josh a cup of water."

Gently, she lifted his head and touched the cool rim of the metal cup to his lips. Josh drank greedily, savoring the cool water. "W-what happened?" he managed to croak.

"That's what we want to know, partner. We found you on the edge of Rica Creek. Simon was gone, hauled off by what looks like Comancheros."

Josh squeezed his eyes shut, trying to force the thoughts tumbling through his head into some order that made sense. Gingerly, he touched the bandage on the side of his head.

"You remember anything?" Marylee whispered.

Slowly, his thoughts began to sort themselves. "We spotted the cows on the caprock." He hesitated, trying to remember what happened next. "I'd no sooner started across the creek than my dun stumbled. Then something hit me, and that's all I remember." He licked his lips.

"Here. Take another drink," said Marylee, lifting his head slightly.

He gulped the rest of the water and leaned back. "Thanks." He just wanted to sleep, but something nagged at him, something Tiny had said about Simon.

Marylee handed the empty cup to Luke. "More water, Luke."

Josh licked his lips. "What . . . was it you said about Simon? Is the boy all right?"

"He's gone, partner. The Comancheros kidnapped him."

Josh stared at the tall man looking down at him. Slowly, Tiny's words shouldered their way through the jumbled thoughts in his skull. He struggled to sit up.

"No. You need your rest," said Marylee, trying to hold him down.

He pushed her hand aside and threw his legs over the side of the bed. "I can rest later," he muttered, sitting on the edge of the bed. "It's Simon we've got to worry about now. We—"

Luke came running back into the bedroom clutching a soiled piece of paper in his hand. "Josh! Look! It's from the Comancheros." He handed the paper to Josh.

Marylee gasped. "What does it say?"

Josh blinked at the words, but they seemed to run together. "Here, Tiny. You read it."

The big man cleared his throat and read the words scribbled on the wrinkled sheet of paper. "Gold for boy." Tiny looked up. "That's all it says, Josh. Gold for boy."

Josh looked at the young boy. "Where did you find this, Luke?"

"When I was pumping the water at the sink. I thought I heard something at the door. When I opened it, this was lying on the ground with a rock on it."

"Did you see anybody out there?"

The youth shook his head. "Too dark."

Marylee's eyes grew wide in alarm. "But, how can we do what the note says? We don't know where the gold is, or even if it exists."

"It's here, and I got a feeling it's close, but you're right. We have nothing to exchange for Simon." Josh leaned forward and clutched his head to still the pounding. His stomach churned.

Tiny's face grew grim. "So what do you reckon to do, Josh?"

Without looking up, he muttered, "We've got to take him back."

Tiny whistled. "You're biting off a mighty big chunk of steak, partner. You sure we're not going to choke on it?"

Wincing against the pain in his head, Josh looked up. "Not if we play our cards right." He glanced at Luke. "How about saddling my dun, son. If I can talk your sister into wrapping me some cold biscuits in oil-cloth, I'm going to take a little ride." He started to rise.

"Forget it, Josh," growled Tiny, gently pushing the woozy cowpoke back on the bed. "You're weaker than a fresh-thrown calf. If there's any riding to be done, I'll do it."

Josh sagged back, too weak to attempt to rise again and too tired to argue.

"Whereabouts was you planning on riding to?"

Forcing a faint grin, the lanky cowboy replied, "Atascocita. Wake Frenchy up. Bring back a few sticks of that dynamite and fuses we hauled back from Dodge City."

"Dynamite!" Marylee exclaimed. "What on earth for?"

Tiny just grinned at Josh. "Don't worry, partner. "I'll smoke up the road. Back in a couple hours." He grabbed his hat. "Come on, Luke. Help me saddle up."

After Tiny and Luke left, Marylee turned to Josh with a frown on her slender face. "What are you going to do with the dynamite? It's nothing to fool with."

He dragged the tip of his tongue across his dry lips and lay back on the bed. "I reckon you're right, Miss Marylee. I'm tired as a neck-wrung rooster."

With a warm smile, she laid her hand on his arm. "I'll bring you a bowl of hot beef stew. It'll perk you right up."

After putting himself around a few mouthfuls of belly-warming stew, Josh dropped into a deep sleep, not even awakening when Tiny returned with the dynamite.

Around the breakfast table next morning, despite a pounding headache, Josh laid out his plan. "First, Archiveque or one of his men had to see you haul my carcass back here yesterday. They figured I was dead, so you got no choice but to bury me. They'll be watching, and they'll figure they got one less cow-poke to worry about. I'll stay hidden in here today, and tonight, with the dynamite, I'll slip out and find them." He grinned at Marylee. "And I'll bring your brother back. That's a promise."

Luke coughed. "But, won't they be watching the house like they've been doing?"

Tiny chuckled. "They figure they got us between the rock and the hard place, boy. With one of us dead, they won't figure they got much to worry about." The big man shrugged his massive shoulders and frowned at Josh. "Only one thing I don't like about it."

"What's that?" the lanky cowpoke asked while chewing a mouthful of fried bacon.

With a crooked grin on his square face, Tiny chucked. "I got to get out there and dig a grave, and the day looks like a hot one."

They all laughed.

Chapter Twenty-two

Mid-morning, Tiny and Luke, followed by Marylee, hauled a sheet wrapped around a bundle of blankets to the grave beyond the barn. Tiny couldn't help grinning. "Make it look like we're having a hard time carrying him, boy."

Marylee hurried forward and took one corner of the sheet from Luke. "This should help convince them," she whispered.

Fifteen minutes later, Tiny packed the dirt over the grave and Luke stuck a wooden cross at the head of the mound. They bowed their heads. "I ain't no good on praying," muttered Tiny, "but right now I'm praying like a hard-shell deacon that them Comancheros fall for this little show of ours."

* * *

Two hours later, a lone rider came down from the caprock to the north. "Who is it, do you think?" Marylee whispered as she and Josh peered through the kitchen window at the rider who was still half a mile distant.

For a moment, Josh's vision blurred. He blinked once or twice, clearing it. "I'm guessing it's one of Archiveque's Comancheros coming to set up a meeting to exchange Simon for the gold."

She looked up at him in alarm. "What are we going to tell him?"

Josh grinned at her. "Go out to the barn and let Tiny and Luke know this old boy is coming. Have Tiny tell him that they should come tomorrow when the sun is straight overhead. We need time to bring the gold in."

Ten minutes later, he watched from a gunport in one of the bedroom window shutters while Tiny and Luke stood in the open door to the barn and palavered with a sneering Comanchero astride a handsome dapple-gray gelding.

The Comanchero pointed to the fresh grave, then made a threatening throat-slitting gesture.

Tiny simply nodded, and the leering Mexican wheeled the dapple-gray around, and with a curious glance at the main house, dug his fist-sized rowels into the horse's flanks and raced across the valley to the caprock.

"What would we have done if he had wanted to search the house just to make sure you were dead?"

Josh nodded to the bedroom. "There's always the cellar."

Violent thunderstorms, spawned by hot air rising off the prairie into the cool atmosphere, exploded late that afternoon, deluging the countryside with a driving rain, bringing an early darkness to the valley, a darkness that was shattered from time to time by thunderous bolts of lightning.

While there was still light, Josh had sent Luke to saddle his dun while he rolled half a dozen sticks of fused dynamite in oilcloth and tied the bundle snugly before stuffing it in his saddlebags.

Tiny packed .44 ammunition into the other pouch of the saddlebags. He glanced at Josh from under his eyebrows. "How's the head, partner?"

"Good. Sore, but good," the lanky cowpoke replied, not wanting to admit that from time to time throughout the day, a wave of dizziness had swept over him. He changed the subject. "This storm couldn't have come at a better time. If anyone up there was watching, the rain drove them inside."

He threw the bags over his shoulder and reached for

his Winchester. He grinned at Marylee, her face pale and drawn. "See you in the morning with the boy."

An hour later, Josh topped out on the caprock a few miles west of the network of washes he had explored a few days earlier. The rain continued to fall and the lightning to explode as he turned east, angling for the Comanchero camp.

Within thirty minutes, the storm passed and the waning moon came out from behind the clouds. Ahead, Josh spotted the faint glow of firelight. Dismounting, he ground-reined his dun and, six-gun in hand, crept forward, his boots ankle-deep in runoff water. As he drew closer to the glow, he heard laughter.

Dropping to his belly, he eased to the rim of the wash.

Below, the Comancheros were high and dry in their wagons, while water swirled around their wagon wheels. Laughter and curses came from the wagons as the Comancheros drank themselves into a stupor.

Josh studied the odd collection of wagons before settling on a celerity with a red oilcloth top, the fanciest of all the buggies, ambulances, and freight wagons about the camp. Even as he watched, Archiveque stuck his head out through the flap, then ducked back inside.

Moments later, Simon stumbled out. Archiveque followed, remaining under the oilcloth canopy while Simon slogged through the water and mud to slice off a slab of beef from the roasting hindquarter.

Resisting the impulse to put a hole between the Comanchero's eyes, Josh remained motionless, looking on as Simon, his clothes stained and ripped, returned with the broiled meat.

Later, after the camp drifted into drunken slumber, Josh brought his dun closer and retrieved three sticks of dynamite from the saddlebags. On one of the fuses, he clipped off all but two inches.

Suddenly, his vision blurred and his head swam. He grabbed the saddle horn to steady himself. He drew a deep breath, filling his lungs with fresh, clean oxygen. After a few moments, the dizziness passed.

Dropping into a crouch, he slipped around to the rear of the camp and slid down the wash to come up behind Archiveque's celerity wagon. A lamp burned inside. Josh listened intently, hearing Archiveque's snoring and a faint snuffling.

Lifting the oilcloth slightly, Josh peered inside.

The Comanchero lay on his back on a wooden cot, his mouth gaping open, and snoring like a cross-cut saw.

Simon was hunkered in one corner of the wagon, his ankles and wrists bound. His eyes grew wide when he spotted Josh, who quickly touched his finger to his lips. Simon nodded.

Moving carefully, Josh climbed into the rear of the celerity, keeping the muzzle of his .44 Colt aimed at Archiveque's gaping mouth. With his free hand, he sliced the youth's bonds, then jammed the muzzle of his six-gun into the Comanchero's mouth.

Gagging and sputtering, the fat Comanchero flailed his arms and legs in an effort to roll off his cot, but Josh's icy warning stayed him. "One more move and you're dead."

Archiveque froze, staring up at Josh in fear.

In a low voice, Josh said, "Now, roll over and put your hands behind you, real slow. One wrong move and you're a dead man."

The fear in the Comanchero's eyes turned into a look of arrogance. "Hey, *gringo,* you fool Archiveque. You not *muerto.*"

"Maybe not, but you will be if you don't do exactly what I tell you. Now roll over."

Glaring malevolently up at Josh, Archiveque did as he was told. "Tie him up good, Simon," Josh said, his finger tight on the trigger.

When the boy finished, he looked up, his eyes

hard and cold. "This is the butcher who killed Matt and John. We ought to give him a taste of his own medicine."

Josh studied the boy a moment. "Later. We need him to get us out of here. Then we'll worry about what to do with him."

The muscles in the young boy's jaw stood out like whipcord. "I know what I want to do to him."

Josh jammed the muzzle in the middle of the fat Comanchero's back. "Now, Simon, go out to the fire and bring me back a torch."

The young boy frowned at him.

"A torch, a burning branch. And hurry."

He pulled the muzzle from the Mexican's back. "Now, roll over and stand up.

"You never leave this place alive, *gringo,*" Archiveque muttered as he turned over. "There are too many, and you are only one."

By the time Simon returned, Archiveque had struggled to his feet.

His eyes narrowing, Josh pulled out the short-fused dynamite and jammed it under the dirty red sash encircling the Mexican's broad belly.

The Mexican's eyes grew wide. A faint groan sounded in his fat throat.

Josh took the torch and with a cruel laugh, said, "I see you understand what I'm planning on doing,

Archiveque. I might only be one, but I guarantee you, I'm enough. And if I'm not, you won't be around to notice." He gestured to the front. "Now, out. Simon, you go first."

Reluctantly, the Comanchero shuffled through the flap in the oilcloth after the young boy and stopped under the canopy behind the wagon seat.

A sneer curled his thick lips. "How does the *gringo* think I will get down with my hands tied?"

"That's easy," Josh replied, removing the stick of dynamite and then kicking Archiveque in the small of the back, sending him screaming and spinning off the wagon to the muddy ground. "That's how," the lanky cowpoke growled, leaping to the ground and jerking Archiveque to his feet and jamming the dynamite back under the Comanchero's sash before the commotion drew his men from their wagons.

Still half asleep, the rest of the Comancheros poured from their wagons like cockroaches. Josh fired into the air and then held the burning branch within inches of the dynamite under the stunned Comanchero's belly. "One shot, and they'll be picking up pieces of you all over their wagons."

"No," the frightened leader called to his men. "Do nothing. Listen to what the *gringo* says."

At that moment, Rynning and Mad Tom, still half drunk, staggered from one of the army ambulances.

"What the—" Rynning's eyes grew hard. "You," he snarled.

Josh's eyes narrowed. "I suspected Leach was in cahoots with these polecats. Now I'm certain."

Rynning looked around. A dozen Comancheros were glaring murderously at Josh. "You ain't getting out of here, cowboy."

"You're wrong, Rynning. I'm getting out of here, and I'm taking the boy and Archiveque with me. And then, I'm coming for you. You can tell Leach I said so." He moved the brightly burning torch closer to the dynamite. "Want to argue?"

"Shut up, Rynning," shouted Archiveque. "Do what the *gringo* say."

"I want two horses, saddled. And now." Josh glared at Archiveque. "You're going with us."

The Comanchero leader stared at him defiantly. "You tell them."

Josh slammed the muzzle of his Colt across the fat Comanchero's nose, breaking it. Blood squirted out. "Now tell them to get the horses."

With blood pouring down his chest, the subdued Mexican nodded to one of his men, who immediately disappeared into the night.

"In the meantime," Josh growled, "the rest of you just squat yourself down around the fire, and nobody will get hurt."

Rynning remained standing. He glared defiantly. "You ain't going to blow him up. You'll go with him."

With a weary grin, Josh pulled out another stick of dynamite and touched the torch to it, then promptly tossed it under the ambulance behind Rynning. In the same motion, he ducked behind the celerity and pulled Simon with him.

The startled gunfighter yelped, took off running, and then made a headfirst dive under a freight wagon moments before the dynamite exploded, obliterating the ambulance and setting off a series of cartridges in the wagon.

After the explosions subsided, Josh whistled for his pony. Just as his dun trotted up, the Mexican returned with two horses, both wild-eyed at the explosion and the gunfire.

Mounting his pony, Josh eyed the Comancheros. "Keep those hoglegs holstered, boys. First shot I hear, Archiveque's dead." He nodded to Simon, who took the lead out of camp. When they reached the first bend in the wash, Josh wheeled the dun about and promptly tossed two more sticks of dynamite into the camp, rocking it with more explosions.

Horses whinnied and squealed. Suddenly a dozen horses, all without saddles, scrambled up the bank of the wash and burst onto the caprock, scattering in every direction.

Taking the reins to the Comanchero's horse, Josh headed back to the ranch, figuring it would be at least an hour before there was any pursuit. "You okay, Simon?"

The young boy looked up, a grin on his slender face. "A lot better now than I was a few minutes ago."

As they rode, Archiveque desperately worked his wrists, rubbing them raw in an effort to loosen his bonds. Slowly, the rope grew slack. He kept his black eyes on the *gringo,* a growing rage blazing in his heaving chest.

The only weapons he now possessed, he told himself, were his hands and teeth, but that would be enough. He would tear the *gringo*'s throat out with his teeth.

Chapter Twenty-three

The ropes about Archiveque's wrists fell away as they approached the rim of the caprock and the trail leading down to Rica Creek. Slyly he eased his horse closer to the *gringo*'s, waiting until the unsuspecting cowboy looked away.

He saw his time, and, with a roar of rage, the savage Comanchero leaped from his saddle, engulfing Josh in his thick arms and sending them both sprawling in the mud.

"Now, I kill you, *gringo*," he growled, scrabbling on his hands and knees for Josh.

The lanky cowpoke rolled onto his side and kicked out with his boot, catching the surprised Comanchero in the side of the head. In the same mo-

229

tion, Josh grabbed for his six-gun, but his fingers grasped an empty holster.

Archiveque grunted, then jumped to his feet, surprising Josh with his agility. With a feral cry, he rushed the lanky cowpoke, wrapping his arms around him, pinning Josh's arms to his sides and jerking the struggling cowboy off his feet.

Clenching his teeth, Josh slammed his forehead into the Mexican's broken nose, eliciting a scream of pain as Archiveque dropped Josh and grabbed his nose.

Josh planted his feet and threw a straight right at the Comanchero's grizzled chin. Archiveque's head snapped back, but he shrugged the blow off and charged Josh, swinging his heavy arms in wild roundhouses.

A ham-sized fist caught Josh on the temple, sending him sprawling to the ground near the edge of the rim, below which was a precipitous hundred-foot drop. Josh's head spun, and his vision blurred. He squeezed his eyes shut.

A high-pitched voice cut through the fog in his head. "Josh! Watch out."

The lanky cowpoke rolled away from the rim a split second before a leering Sosthenes Archiveque slammed his boot heel into the ground where Josh's head had been.

"Josh," Simon called out again.

Struggling to his feet, Josh glared at the leering Comanchero. In the dim light of the waning moon, Josh glimpsed the smug sneer on Archiveque's face as the big Mexican slowly lumbered toward Josh. "Get out of here, Simon," he yelled, doubling his fists and desperately trying to clear his head, waiting for Archiveque's next move. "Ride. Get back to the ranch."

"But Josh—"

"Do it! Now!"

Simon's horse grunted as the boy dug his heels into the animal's flanks, and as the hoofbeats faded into the night, Josh slowly circled the big Mexican, grinning up at him. "Just you and me now, you scavenging murderer."

Pumping his thick fists back and forth, Archiveque bared his blackened teeth. "After I kill you, *gringo,* Archiveque, he take boy back." With a savage roar, he leaped at Josh, who stepped aside and threw a left into the Mexican's cheek, splitting it open.

Archiveque buried his face in the mud and came up sputtering and slung a handful of mud in Josh's face, blinding the lanky cowpoke just long enough for the burly Comanchero to drive him the ground with his shoulder and begin pounding him with his ham-sized fists.

Josh grabbed the lapels of Archiveque's jacket and

jerked forward, yanking the off-balance Comanchero over Josh's head. Quickly, the wiry cowpoke jumped to his feet. Archiveque waded into him, his fists pumping.

Josh fought back, pounding the Comanchero's belly with blistering hooks that the fat man gave no sign of feeling. Josh's breathing grew labored, his leaden arms grew heavy. Slowly, he gave ground as the larger man pounded him toward the rim of the caprock.

"You die now, *gringo*," growled Archiveque, leaning into the smaller man and hammering his fists like pile drivers into Josh's stomach and chest.

Summoning his last measure of strength, Josh clenched his teeth, grabbed Archiveque by the sash and jerked him forward, spinning him around in the same motion. From deep inside him came a final burst of adrenaline. Josh ripped the big Comanchero with a series of right and left crosses, splitting the taller man's other cheek, opening gashes in the swarthy skin on his forehead, smashing his pulpy nose from one side to the other, driving him back.

Suddenly, Archiveque froze, his eyes wide with fear as the caprock rim crumbled under him. He windmilled his arms in a desperate effort to maintain his balance. He opened his lips to scream, but no sound emerged.

He plummeted to the rocks below soundlessly.

For several minutes, Josh stood numbly, staring down into the darkness below. Woodenly, he turned and searched for his Colt.

Despite his bleeding cuts and sore muscles, Josh paused at the base of the trail to climb among the rocks to Archiveque's body.

His fat carcass lay on its back over a boulder. The impact appeared to have broken his spine, but if that didn't kill the Comanchero, then the hole in his skull from which his brains were leaking surely did.

Tiny and Simon met Josh a few miles from the ranch. Tiny whistled softly when he saw his partner's swollen face. "I'd have given a month's pay to see that fight, partner."

Josh forced a crooked grin. "And I'd have given a month's wages if it had been you instead of me, partner."

Back at the ranch, a frantic Marylee tended Josh's cuts and bruises while he related the details of the fight through swollen lips.

Wearing a crooked grin, Tiny looked down at his partner and with a wry touch of humor said, "You look like you been caught in a stampede of buffalo."

Josh looked up with a half-closed eye. "That's exactly how I feel, too."

Luke growled. "It does me good to hear that Mexican scum is dead. I hope he suffered."

Marylee shot a warning look at her brother. "Don't talk like that, Luke."

"If he did," Josh replied, "I don't reckon it was for long."

"Reckon Frenchy'll be glad to hear Archiveque is dead," Tiny observed.

"You know something," Simon whispered, staring unseeing at the shuttered window over the sink. "I thought I would feel good when John and Matt's killers got what they deserved, but I don't feel much different."

Marylee daubed Josh's cuts with coal oil. He winced. "That stings."

She shook her head. "Don't be such a baby."

The boys laughed.

Tiny grew serious. "You know what's coming next, don't you, pard?"

Nodding slowly, Josh muttered, "Afraid so."

Marylee paused in tending Josh. She looked from one to the other, a puzzled frown on her forehead. "What are you talking about? What's coming? Isn't it all over now?"

Josh shook his head briefly. "No."

"But, he's dead. The one responsible for the deaths of my brothers is dead."

"He's dead, but not the others. Those yahoos want the gold as much as Archiveque."

The slender woman's eyes grew wide. She pressed a tiny hand to her lips. "You mean, there's going to be more killing?"

"As sure as you're standing there."

His cigar dangling from his thick lips, Cullen Leach stared up at Rynning in disbelief from behind his desk. "Archiveque's what?"

Rynning touched a match to his cigarette. "Dead. They found him at the bottom of the caprock, his back broke and his head busted open."

Leach cursed. He glared at Mad Tom and Rynning though narrowed eyes. "And where were you two when all of this was happening?"

Mad Tom shuffled his boots nervously. "We was hunting our horses, Mr. Leach. That jasper run them off."

Leach's face grew red. The veins on his neck bulged. "And you just stood there and let him?"

In a cool, sneering voice, Dave Rynning replied, "There was nothing we could do about it. And nothing you could have done about it even if you'd been there, Mr. Leach," he added, a slight trace of defiance edging his words.

The corpulent businessman's eyes blazed. "Maybe

not, but I can do something about it now." He pulled a metal box from the bottom drawer. From it, he counted out a sheath of greenbacks. "I want you to hire half a dozen men and wipe the ranch out."

Mad Tom gaped. "You mean, kill them all? The woman too? The kids?"

Leach just stared at him, his cold, black eyes giving Mad Tom the answer to his question.

"Maybe we should hold off a day or so, Mr. Leach," Rynning suggested in a cool voice. "From what I could make out of all that Mexican jabbering back at their camp, them Mexican boys is going to hit the ranch tonight." He shrugged and gave Leach a conspiratorial grin. "They might just take care of the job for you."

"Hmm." Leach pondered Rynning's suggestion. "Tonight, you say?"

"That's what I heard. Of course, you know them Mex's. *Mañana*. Always *mañana*."

Leach nodded emphatically. "All right. We'll do it your way. Let's see what happens tonight, but—" He jabbed the cigar at Rynning, "if they don't take care of that bunch, then you do the job, or don't come back here. You understand me, both of you?"

Chapter Twenty-four

After Marylee lightly daubed coal oil on the last cut on Josh's forehead, she straightened up and drew a deep breath. "There. That's the last of them. Now, you need to get some rest."

Painfully, Josh pushed himself up from the edge of the bed. "There's no time." He met Tiny's questioning look and nodded. "We've got to get a proper welcome ready for our visitors."

"We've got the firepower," Tiny said, nodding to the cellar below the house. "You got anything in particular in mind?"

Josh shucked his Colt, eyeing the caked mud with distaste. He brushed at it. "Yeah. I got something particular in mind." He jammed the six-gun back in the holster. "Let's get it done."

Simon's high-pitched voice trembled with apprehension. "When do you think they'll hit?"

The lanky cowpoke studied the two nervous boys facing him. "Hard to say. I don't figure they'll come in during the day. They're cowards that don't take on anyone face-to-face, so chances are they'll come in tonight before the moon rises." He paused, a pitiless smile tightening his lips. "And we'll be ready for them."

"Then let's us get busy," Tiny said.

The next two hours, they hauled rifles and ammunition up from the cellar and stacked the supplies at the base of the ladder leading to the roof. Upon moving a case of ammunition from a shelf, Josh noted the adobe on the rock wall appeared fresher than the surrounding adobe coat that was beginning to crack.

At that moment, Luke asked, "Why not carry the rifles on up to the roof now?"

Josh forgot about the wall. "They probably have someone watching. We don't want to show our hand. When it gets to be dusk, we'll haul our gear up."

While Tiny and Simon carried the supplies from the cellar, Josh showed Marylee how to insert fuses into the dynamite. At first, she refused, fearful the cylindrical sticks would explode if she touched them.

Josh laughed. "Don't fret," he said, nodding to the stick in his hand. "Like this, they're harmless. They need a spark." To emphasize his point, he dropped a stick on the floor.

Marylee gasped in surprise, and then a slow smile played over her lips. "All right. Show me what to do."

Josh and Luke went to the barn, leaving Marylee fusing the dynamite. While Josh closed the back doors and dropped the lockbars in place, Luke rolled up three coils of rope as Josh had instructed. "Tonight," the lanky cowpoke had explained, pointing at the hitching rail in from of the barn, "we'll string it from there to the hitching rail in front of the house. Tighter than a cinch strap. I figure they plan on sweeping through here as fast as they can, shooting at the plaza. These ropes might not stop them, but I reckon it'll slow those yahoos down enough for us to make them mighty unhappy with their lot."

Luke grinned. "Yes, sir."

During the afternoon, a blanket of clouds moved in, a portent of coming weather. Later on that afternoon, Josh stepped back and surveyed their work. The Winchesters, all six, were fully loaded and twice as many shoulder belts were filled with spare cartridges. Absently, he shucked his freshly cleaned Colt and spun the full cylinder, feeling a sense of well-being from the purring clicks of the cylinder as it rotated in the frame of the Colt.

From the kitchen, Marylee called, "Fresh coffee.

Venison and gravy will be ready in a few minutes. Biscuits are hot now."

"Sounds good to me," yelped Tiny, hurrying from the bedroom. "Come on, partner."

Josh paused in the doorway to the kitchen, studying the young woman placing platters of steaming venison, hot biscuits, and thick red-eye gravy on the table. Had she not expressed her intentions clearly a few days earlier, he would have thought she was beginning to accommodate herself to the western life.

She glanced at Josh, catching him staring at her. She hesitated, a puzzled frown on her face. She brushed a lock of hair from her eyes. "Something wrong?"

Embarrassed, he ducked his head. "No. Ah—just thinking," he mumbled. "Just thinking," which wasn't a lie, he told himself as he slid in at the table. He was thinking—about Marylee Gaston.

The young woman watched him with her dark eyes, and as he reached for a plate, a small smile played over her lips, and a little thrill of magic filled her heart, a thrill she had never before experienced, not even with her fiancé, Oliver Van Dort.

Up on the caprock, hidden in a wash a short distance from the trail leading down to the valley, Dave Rynning and Mad Tom Gristy watched the Comancheros descend into the valley. "Reckon we'll give them a few minutes, and then ride on down to make sure the whole job's taken care of," Rynning muttered.

Mad Tom shook his head. "I still ain't hankering to kill no woman or kids. It just don't seem right."

Rynning sneered. "Then don't. If them Comancheros don't take care of them, I'll do it. It don't bother me none."

"It's about time," Tiny announced later, opening a window shutter and peering into the growing dusk. "Still cloudy in patches."

"That's one thing in our favor," Josh muttered.

The door burst open and Luke came running in. "Josh, Josh! They're coming." He pointed out the window. "Coming down off the caprock right now."

Josh leaped to his feet. "Luke, tie the ropes tight, just like we talked about this morning. Tiny, Simon, start handing the guns up to me," he ordered, running into the bedroom. Just before he shinnied up the ladder to the roof, he called Marylee. "Make sure the lock bars are on all the shutters."

She called back. "What about the lanterns? You want me to blow them out?"

"No. Leave them on. Let those *hombres* think we're just sitting around knitting and drinking coffee."

On the roof, Josh peered into the darkening night. It the distance, he made out a group of riders, but they were so bunched together, he couldn't tell just how many.

Within a few minutes, the small band of defenders was ready, stationed around the perimeter of the roof. "Don't stand up," Josh warned the boys. "Stay on your knees behind the wall. They'll have to shoot up. As long as the clouds hold, it'll be dark, and if you stay low, they won't see you. If Luke and me did it right, they oughta bunch up down in those ropes. Just shoot into that cluster. That's where Tiny and me will be throwing the dynamite."

By now darkness had settled over the valley. Josh couldn't make out the expressions on the faces of the two boys, but he knew they were scared. He couldn't blame them. He was scared also. "Just do what we say, boys. Scum like these got no belly for a real fight." He glanced at Marylee, who appeared only as a nebulous figure in the dark. "You all right?"

"Yes," she whispered in a breaking voice.

In a loud whisper, Josh called out to Tiny. "You and that Spencer ready to go, partner?"

"Yep. Reckon so, and I got me a handful of loaded tubes in my back pocket." He chuckled. "Why, these unlucky fools is going to think they done run into a whole hibernating den of grizzly bears." He paused, then in a serious tone, added, "Take care, partner. There's still a whole heap of poker games out there for you."

A flood of emotion welled in Josh's chest. He nodded, and in a brusque voice replied, "You too. Don't forget, I got to have you around to bail me out when I get in over my head."

A piercing shout broke the silence of the dark night, followed by a fusillade of gunfire and the pounding of hooves. Slugs hummed through the air, splatting into the adobe and rock building.

Squinting into the darkness, Josh cautioned them through clenched teeth. "Remember! Keep your heads down."

The thunder of hammering hooves grew closer, giving no sign of slowing. Josh grinned to himself. *That's it, boys. Keep those cayuses of yours at a full gallop.*

The Comancheros swept in. Slugs thudded into the heavy wooden shutters covering the windows, smashed into the thick slab door in front.

Suddenly a horse squealed and a voice cursed. In the next instant, in the midst of a cacophony of whinnying and squealing came the sickening thud of thousand-pound animals slamming into one another.

"Now!" Josh shouted, and from the rooftop, Winchesters cracked even as the old Spencer bellowed and spat out its three hundred and fifty grains of lead.

The darkness below between the main house and barn was lit only by faint beams of light from the gunports in the shutters. Josh emptied his Winchester into the milling crowd and then grabbed a stick of dynamite.

A guttural cry echoed above the squealing horses and cursing Comancheros. "*La emboscada!* Ambush. *Corra! Salga de aqui!*" Josh recognized enough Tex-Mex to know their leader was telling them to run, to get out there.

"Maybe this will help you make up your minds, boys," he muttered, tossing a burning stick of dynamite into the melee below.

Exploding dynamite lit the night, revealing the terrified faces of Comancheros desperate to untangle themselves and escape into the safety of the darkness.

"Josh!" Marylee screamed. "The trapdoor!"

The lanky cowpoke spun in time to see a Comanchero stick his head above the roof. Tiny's .44 Remington belched a plume of yellow and the Comanchero dropped back into the house. "I'll take care of below," the big cowpoke called out, disappearing through the trapdoor.

Suddenly, a powerful blow struck Josh on his left shoulder, spinning him around and sending him sprawling on the roof. He grimaced and muttered a curse as he struggled back to his feet. The slug had caught the meaty part of his shoulder, breaking no bones, but burning like the blue fires of Hades.

From the hardpan below came cries of pain and the pounding of hooves as the Comancheros fled the ambush. Even as the hammering of hooves faded into the night, gunshots came from the kitchen. "Stay here," Josh shouted, racing across the roof. "Call out if they come back." Hastily he clambered down the ladder, grimacing at the pain emanating from his shoulder.

Acrid gunsmoke filled the house. He raced into the kitchen where three dead Comancheros lay in puddles of blood on the floor.

Tiny was slumped back against the table, a crooked grin on his square face and a Bowie knife sticking out his belly. With a grimace, he parted his lips and whispered in a thin voice, "Reckon—you— you best stay away from them poker games, partner. It don't look like I'll be around to pull your bacon out of the fire no more." His eyelids fluttered, then closed, and his broad chin dropped to his chest.

Rynning and Gristy had watched in disbelief at the intensity of the firepower directed at the Comancheros. When the dynamite began exploding, Rynning shook his head and grunted. "Reckon it's going to be up to us now. Let's get back to Atascocita and tell Leach."

Chapter Twenty-five

A great roaring filled Josh's ears, deafening him. He stared in disbelief at his partner's limp body while Marylee pressed an ear to Tiny's chest. Slowly, without lifting her head, she turned her eyes to Josh and shook her head. Her eyes grew wide when she spotted Josh's bloody shoulder.

She rose to his side. "You've been shot."

Josh bit his bottom lip and tears filled his eyes. Ignoring her concern for his shoulder, he nodded to the boys. "Give me a hand here. Let's carry him to the bedroom." Gently, they laid Tiny on the feather-down bed.

Josh stepped back, his jaw set, his eyes grim as a deadly resolve surged through his veins. Despite the pain in his shoulder, he shucked his Colt, filling the

246

chambers with fresh cartridges. "Luke, saddle my horse."

Marylee gasped. "What are you doing? You can't go anywhere. You've been shot. You need to be taken care of."

He ignored her plea. "Simon, get me a Winchester." When the youth left the room, he turned to Marylee. "If I don't make it back, bury Tiny in the grave he dug. His full name was Luther Frank Hamilton, great-grandson of Alexander Hamilton, and he was born in Injun Bayou over in East Texas."

"But, where are you going? What are you going to do?"

His gray eyes turned to ice. "I'm going to make sure Tiny didn't die for nothing."

Her face grew hard. "You're going after Leach, aren't you?"

"Yes," he replied, his face like granite. "Leach is behind all the trouble around here. Him and Archiveque was thicker than flies on a sore."

"Here you are, Josh," said Simon, handing the lanky cowpoke the Winchester.

"Simon, you and Luke load up the dead Comancheros and haul them away from here. Were it me, I'd leave them for the vultures, but Tiny would bury them. So I reckon you best find a spot and plant them."

Marylee grabbed his arm as he turned to leave. "Josh, don't. There's too many of them. If Leach wants this place, I'll let him have it. It isn't worth dying over."

The lean cowpoke looked down at her. "You don't really believe that."

She met his steady gaze, then lowered her eyes and slowly shook her head. "No, but I'm scared."

Josh grinned and laid his hand on her arm. "I'm scared too, but after tonight, you won't have to worry about Cullen Leach anymore."

Fists pounding at the door awakened Cullen Leach, whose living quarters were in the rear of the C. L. Freight Company. Muttering a curse, the corpulent businessman rolled out of bed and lit a lantern. He uttered another curse when he opened the door and saw Rynning and Gristy. "What is it?"

Rynning explained. "Them Comancheros didn't do the job, Leach. I reckon we've got to hire some gunnies after all."

Nodding, Leach stepped back. "I figured it would come to this. The only way to make sure a thing is done is to do it yourself. Come on in. We'll go up front, and I'll get the money to pay them."

* * *

Across the street, Winchester in hand, Josh stood in the darkened livery relating the events of the night to Frenchy and George Buckalew, the latter wearing bright red longjohns. Tears welled in Frenchy's eyes. She tugged her housecoat tighter about her thick waist. "Tiny, he was a good boy," she whispered in a frail voice.

"That he was," George echoed.

Josh chewed on his bottom lip.

Frenchy shook her head. "Bad time though. Sheriff Ellis is out of town."

A crooked grin played over Josh's lips. "Maybe not."

His eyes met hers, and, understanding his cryptic reply, she smiled. "Reckon you're right. It might be a good time."

"Look at that," George exclaimed in a crackling voice. "The lights come on over to Leach's place."

Eyeing the lit window with cold determination, Josh said, "That's why I come to you." He pointed the Winchester at the freight office. "George, I want you to go over and tell Leach I'm coming for him. I'm coming for him and his hired guns tonight, and that there's no chance in Hades that none of them will see the sun rise this morning."

The old man cackled. "Be right happy to."

"No," interrupted Frenchy. "I want to do it. I want to see the look on that no-account's face when I tell him that."

George snorted. "Look, old woman. Josh wants a man to do it. That's why he asked me."

"Bull—"

Josh broke in. "Both of you go." He paused. "You two've been mighty good to me and Tiny." He paused and shot a quick glance at C. L. Freight. "If something goes wrong, look after them kids and their sister at the Gaston place. I'd consider it a mighty fine favor."

George's phlegmy eyes brightened. "Don't worry none, son. If you don't get them no-account, sons—"

"George!" Frenchy snapped. "You watch your mouth. We know what you mean."

The old man grinned. "If something happens, and you don't do it all, we'll do the rest. You can depend on that."

Frenchy turned to leave. "Well, old man. If you're going with me, let's go."

"Hold on, woman. I'll get me my hat. I ain't going nowhere half-dressed."

Josh grimaced. While the bleeding had stopped, the pain in his shoulder was intensifying. He fished through his parfleche bag and popped a petal of peyote in his mouth.

*   *   *

Cullen Leach jerked around at the knock on the door of the freight office. "Who the—" He nodded to Mad Tom. "See who that is."

Mad Tom opened the door. His jaw dropped open when he saw Frenchy in her faded chenille house robe and George in his red long johns and wearing a hat. He finally found his tongue. "Whatever it is, Mr. Leach ain't seeing nobody ton—"

"Move over, boy," snapped Frenchy, pushing by the surprised gunman. With George right behind her, she came to a halt in front of Leach's desk. She stared at the stack of greenbacks in his hand, then gave Dave Rynning a look of disgust. "Paying off your killers in the middle of the night, Cullen?"

He blustered. "What are you doing here? You got business with me, come back during business hours."

Frenchy sneered. "I ain't got business with you. It's Josh Carson that's got business, and he means to collect. He's across the street now, and he said to tell you—" She paused and, looking at Rynning and Gristy like they were lower than a snake's belly, added, "He said to tell you and all of your hired guns that not a one of you is going to see the sun rise in the morning."

Leach's eyes narrowed and a smug grin twisted his fat lips. "You think so, huh?"

George cackled. "I know so."

"Don't be too sure." Leach dragged his tongue over his lips. "That jasper won't be so almighty sure of hisself if I keep you two here."

Frenchy's eyes grew wide, and her nostrils flared in anger. "Not even a lowdown snake like you would do that, Cullen Leach."

He sneered. "No?"

"No!" Mad Tom Gristy stepped forward, his six-gun in hand and cocked. "I don't mind killing, but I don't hold with killing women or kids or even old men. And I reckon that's likely to happen if they stay here. I'm sorry, Mr. Leach, but I ain't going to let you hold these two old folks like that."

"Gristy!" Leach shouted.

Rynning reached for his revolver, but Gristy covered him. "Don't do it, Rynning. You're fast, but not fast enough to beat a cocked hammer." Without taking his eyes off Rynning, he said, "Frenchy, you and George light a shuck out of here. Now."

Chapter Twenty-six

Halfway across the darkened street, gunshots exploded in the freight office. "Run, old man," Frenchy shouted as she ducked and lumbered for the livery. Behind them, a cry of pain filled the air and then drifted away on the faint breeze.

Josh smiled in grim satisfaction from where he was crouched in the shadows between the livery and the blacksmith shop when Frenchy and George reached the safety of the livery. He knew the old couple would immediately arm themselves in case Leach came after them.

The windows in the C. L. Freight office suddenly went dark. Cupping his hand to his mouth, he called out, "Leach! I'm coming after you and your hired guns. You can run, but it won't do no good. I'll track you down wherever you are." He jerked the Winchester to his shoulder and touched off two rounds through the windows.

In the darkened office, Leach and Rynning dropped to the floor when the windows shattered and the slugs smashed into the walls. "Blast that jasper," Leach muttered, rising to his knees behind his desk and pulling his gunbelt from the bottom drawer. Still wearing his house robe and slippers, he strapped the belt around his ample belly. "We got to get him, Rynning. He could ruin everything."

Rynning remained silent, considering his next step. He figured he was on a sinking ship, and the best move he could make was to bail out, head over to New Mexico Territory or farther on to Arizona Territory.

In the distance, he heard the rattling of a buckboard and the whinnying of horses pulling into the livery.

In the next moment, Josh's voice carried through the night. "And you best not be counting on that lily-livered gunhand you got in there with you, Leach. He's a backshooter and spineless coward who never gunned down any jasper facing him."

If Rynning had been undecided as to his next step,

Josh's derisive words made up his mind. "We go out the back door, Leach. You head north. I'll go south. We'll swing around and pin that loud-mouthed cowboy between us and send him to Hades." As a precaution, Rynning slid another six-gun under his belt beneath his vest.

In the livery, Marylee and her brothers jumped down from the buckboard and hurried into the office. George shoved the door open, and they rushed inside.

"Frenchy," exclaimed Marylee. "Where's Josh?"

The older woman shook her head and nodded to the livery. "Out there somewhere. He's going after Leach and his hired guns."

Luke laid his hand on his sister's arm. "Don't worry. He'll be all right."

Uncertain what the gunshots and scream from Leach's office meant, Josh eased backward through the shadows cast by the livery, making his way down the alley. Several mules in the corral looked up at him as he glided past, but then returned to the hay they'd been munching on.

Josh paused at the corner of the corral and studied the dark hulk of the blacksmith's shop next door. He strained his ears for any sound out of the ordinary, but all he heard was the occasional snuffling of the mules in the corral.

At the same time, Rynning was creeping along the far side of the blacksmith's, planning on slipping up to the livery from behind. If he couldn't find Josh Carson, he would take Frenchy and George hostage and make Carson come to him. He paused at the corner of the blacksmith shop.

The hair on the back of Josh's neck bristled as a faint sound beyond the shop reached his ears. He squinted into the shadows cast by the adobe walls of the blacksmith shop. Was it just his imagination? Or was Leach or one of his gunnies on the other side of the shop?

Taking no chances, he slipped through the bottom rails of the corral and hurried to the street where he made his way cautiously along the front of the shop, planning on coming up behind whoever might be there.

He peered around the corner and, realizing he had been holding his breath, took a deep gulp of air and breathed a sigh of relief. *It must have been my imagination,* he told himself, slipping along the wall to the rear of the shop.

He paused at the corner and pressed up against the adobe wall, listening intently. He stiffened as a spur jangled. Dropping into a crouch, Josh started to ease his head around the corner, but before he had a chance to look, a six-gun exploded, and his Stetson flew off his head.

Josh dropped to the ground and fired a single shot blindly up the alley. A sharp curse came on the echo of the gunshot, and Josh rolled into the alley in time to see a shadowy figure slide through the corral rails.

The lanky cowboy jumped to his feet and raced back along the side of the blacksmith shop, planning on cutting off whoever was out there at the street.

Lit by pale moonlight, Rynning sprinted across the corral for the livery office, but before he reached the livery door, two Winchesters opened up in his direction. The startled gunhand leaped aside and pressed up against the clapboard wall next to the open door, cursing his luck, wishing now that he'd followed his first impulse and left this miserable little town behind in his dust.

His head was turned, his eyes on the complete darkness beyond the open door to the livery. Suddenly, Josh's voice froze him. "Hold it, Rynning. One twitch, and you're a dead man."

Slowly Dave Rynning cut his eyes to Josh and grinned. "You said you was going kill me anyway, cowboy. I'll make it easy for you." He opened his fist and his six-gun fell to the ground.

Instinctively, Josh's eyes went to the revolver, giving Rynning time to pull his hideout from under his vest. Before Josh could react, Rynning dropped into a crouch and began firing, emptying the chamber at the wiry cowpoke facing him. A slug slammed into Josh's wounded shoulder, spinning him to the ground where he thumbed off three quick shots at the black-garbed gunhand so rapidly that one report blended with the others.

The leering smirk on Rynning's face vanished when the first slug caught him in the chest, exploding his heart and slamming him back against the livery wall. He didn't feel the next two that punched in behind the first one.

Josh struggled to his feet, his left arm dangling uselessly. He grimaced against the pain. This time, it was broken. He glanced around furtively, figuring he was still facing two guns.

With one hand, he fumbled to reload the Colt. Before he could, another shot rang out, knocking his leg from under him. Josh sprawled in the dust. His Colt flew from his hand.

Looking about desperately, he saw the bulk of Cullen Leach climb through the corral rails and waddle toward him.

Frightened, the mules had gathered by the feed troughs in a shadowy corner of the livery. Pushing himself to his feet, Josh lurched into the livery, forcing his way through the nervous mules. His brain raced.

Without warning, Leach fired into the herd of mules. They brayed and stampeded, leaving Josh alone.

Leach squinted into the small patch of shadows, trying to find Josh. "You're a dead man, cowboy. You played a hand, but it was a loser." He eased closer.

Josh backed up to the feed trough, and then his hand touched the handle of the pitchfork used to fork hay into the trough.

Frantically, he unbuckled his gunbelt, hoping to create enough of a distraction so he could get close enough with the pitchfork.

"Might as well come on out, cowboy," said Leach, peering into the shadows. "I'll find you sooner or later."

Josh remained silent, grimacing against the throbbing in his leg and arm that sent searing pain through every muscle in his body.

Leach took another step.

Josh drew a deep breath and tossed his gunbelt to the far end of the shed. It struck the wall with a clatter. Leach turned and fired three shots at the sound, giving Josh time to grab the pitchfork, but just as he launched it at the corpulent businessman, his leg buckled, sending the wiry cowpoke sprawling to the ground in the moonlight and the pitchfork landing harmlessly in the dirt at Leach' feet.

With a cruel laugh, Leach approached Josh. "Good try, cowboy. But you didn't buck the tiger." He extended his arm and pointed the muzzle of his six-gun at Josh's head. "Say—"

Chapter Twenty-seven

The crack of a Winchester cut off his sentence as a round black hole appeared in his forehead. For a moment, Cullen Leach stood staring in disbelief, and then he crumpled to the ground.

Winchester in hand, Marylee was the first to reach Josh. She knelt at his side, tears in her eyes. Her words ran together. "Are you hurt bad? Here, boys, let's get him inside, and be careful. Get the buckboard. No, we can carry him. I mean, let's—"

Frenchy stopped her. "Calm down, dear, calm down. Let me in there. We'll take care of him, don't you fret. And you, old man, get out the good whiskey. This boy's going to need a few good slugs."

* * *

Next morning, Josh awakened in Frenchy and George's bed, his leg bandaged and his arm in a sling. Marylee was at his side. "Doc Nicholson tended the arm while you were unconscious," she said, fighting back the tears. "He said you would be just fine, but you can't do anything strenuous for a while."

Josh dragged the tip of his tongue over his dry lips. "Leach?"

"Dead," said George.

"Who did it?"

Frenchy and George looked at Marylee. Luke spoke up, his voice filled with pride. "My sister, Josh. She did it."

The lanky cowpoke looked up at her in disbelief. Her eyes blazed fire, and she set her jaw. "Yes, I did it. I didn't want to, but like you told me on the trip down, this is a different kind of world out here, and so I suppose I'll just have to get used to it."

The boys grinned. Frenchy winked at Josh who frowned and mumbled. "Used to it? What about California?"

A wistful look came into her eyes, but then faded. "I'll write Oliver. I've got a ranch to look after, two brothers to look after, and—" She hesitated.

Simon giggled. "Go ahead, Sis. Tell him." Before she could say a word, Simon blurted out, "And maybe a husband to look after."

Marylee sat on the edge of the bed and laid her hand on Josh's arm. "If you want."

Whatever pain had been coursing through his body vanished in euphoria. He grinned. "If I want?" He grinned. "I'll hobble down the aisle on two busted legs if I have to."

Chapter Twenty-eight

They buried Tiny beside Matt and John Gaston the next day.

A week later, Josh hobbled into the kitchen and plopped down at the table. "Good morning, Mrs. Carson," he said with a grin as wide as the Canadian River.

"Good morning to you, Mr. Carson," she said, her eyes twinkling as she poured him a cup of coffee.

At that moment, Simon and Luke came in covered with whitewash. "Almost finished, Sis." Simon grinned. "Those walls will be nice and smooth with no cracks in them."

Josh frowned. "Cracks?"

Luke nodded. "Yep. Sis had complained about the cracks in the whitewash on the bedroom walls. You

264

have to put new coats on the walls to keep them nice and smooth."

Josh stared at them in surprise. "What's that?"

Simon and Luke looked at each other, puzzled. Simon explained. "After a couple years, the heavy coat of whitewash and adobe starts to crack. That's when we have to put another coat on."

"Well, I'll be," Josh muttered, remembering the fresh patch of whitewash on the adobe in the cellar. "I wonder . . ."

Marylee frowned. "Wonder what, Josh? Is something wrong?"

With a chuckle, he said, "I think I might have just figured out where your gold is."

Ten minutes later, a wild yelp from the cellar told him he had guessed right.

NORELIUS COMMUNITY LIBRARY
1403 1st Avenue South
DENISON, IOWA 51442
712-263-9355